W9-AUA-182

MADDY WEST AND THE TONGUE TAKER

MADDY WEST AND THE TONGUE TAKER

BRIAN FALKNER

Illustrated by

DONOVAN BIXLEY

Maddy West and the Tongue Taker
is first published in the United States
by Capstone Young Readers in 2015,
A Capstone Imprint
1710 Roe Crest Drive
North Mankato, Minnesota 56003
www.capstoneyoungreaders.com

Text © 2012 Brian Falkner
Illustrations © 2012 Donovan Bixley

Published by arrangement with Walker Books Australia Pty. Ltd., Sydney.

All rights reserved. No part of this book may be reproduced, transmitted, broadcast or stored in an information retrieval system in any form or by any means, graphic, electronic or mechanical, including photocopying, taping and recording, without written permission of the publisher.

Library of Congress Cataloging-in-Publication Data is available on the Library of Congress website.
ISBN: 978-1-62370-084-3 (paper-over-board)

Summary: Maddy West can speak every language in the world. When she is asked to help translate some ancient scrolls, she is thrilled. But she soon learns that the scrolls hide many secrets . . . secrets that send Maddy on a wild adventure with a stowaway ninja, a mysterious monkey, a Bulgarian wrestler, evil magic, and a fiendish witch. Does Maddy have what it takes to save herself and her new friends?

Image credits: Shutterstock (endsheet pattern)

Printed in China
032014
008081RRDF14

For Annie, with love

Congratulations to the taste-test winners:
Darcy Holdem, Kamo High School,
Whangarei, New Zealand
Jacquie Yee, St. Cuthbert's College,
Auckland, New Zealand
Stephanie Day, The Alexander Dawson School,
Las Vegas, USA
Maddy West, Hatton Vale High School,
Queensland, Australia

And a special congratulations to:
Gabby Head, Wenona School,
Sydney, Australia

CHAPTER ONE

THE DOCTOR

WHEN MADDY STARTED SPEAKING JAPANESE, her mom took her to the doctor.

The doctor was a gentle, gray-haired man with gold-rimmed glasses that made him look intelligent. Maddy liked the doctor immediately.

"So what is the problem today?" the doctor asked, smiling kindly at Maddy.

"She's speaking in foreign tongues," Maddy's mom said, but the word "foreign" had a strange ring to it, as if it brought a bad taste to her mouth when she said it.

The doctor frowned and, for some reason, began to examine Maddy's ear.

"What kind of foreign tongues?" he asked. There was no bad taste to the way he said it.

"Japanese," Maddy's mom said. "At least, I think it was

Japanese. It might have been Korean, or Taiwanese, or even Chinese."

It had been Japanese, but this conversation seemed to be between her mom and the doctor, so Maddy didn't butt in to tell them so.

"So you've been speaking a foreign language?" The doctor raised an eyebrow at Maddy then turned back to her mom. "I don't quite understand. What do you want me to do?"

"I want you to . . ." Maddy's mom stopped. It was quite clear that she wasn't sure what she wanted the doctor to do. "I want you to . . . to . . . to fix her."

The doctor looked from Maddy to her mom, then back again.

"I don't think she's broken," he said. Maddy could have hugged him on the spot.

"Well, I want you to do *some*thing," Maddy's mom said.

"All right," the doctor said. "I suppose we could run some tests."

"Tests, good. Yes, tests," Maddy's mom said.

"Would it be all right if I spoke to Maddy alone for a moment first?" the doctor asked.

"Alone? Why?" Maddy's mom narrowed her eyes. It made her look like a cat.

"I think it will help," the doctor said.

"Oh." Maddy's mom looked sideways at Maddy but stood up. "How long will it take?"

"As long as it takes," the doctor said.

Maddy's mom narrowed her eyes even further at the doctor.

Maddy was starting to like him more and more.

Maddy's mom walked over to the door, opened it, and left.

The doctor stood and closed the door softly.

"What kind of tests?" Maddy asked.

"Oh, there are no tests," the doctor said. "I just said that so your mother would wait outside. I hope you don't mind."

"I thought so," Maddy said with a smile. "And no, I don't mind."

"Now." The doctor sat on the corner of his desk and looked at her over the top of his spectacles. "How old are you, Maddy?"

"I'm nine," Maddy said, "and a half."

"And a very important half it is," the doctor said. "And you speak Japanese? Do you speak any other languages?"

"I don't know," Maddy said. "How many other languages are there?"

"There are hundreds of them," the doctor said. "Too many for any one person to know. I myself learned French at school, and have a little smattering of Polish from my grandmother. I once knew a person who could speak five languages."

Maddy wasn't really listening. She was visualizing a smattering of Polish, which sounded like something that had once happened when she was helping her mom clean the dining table.

"Would you like to hear some French?" the doctor asked. "It's a beautiful language."

"Yes, I honestly would," Maddy replied.

He chuckled. "That's quite extraordinary," he said.

"What is?" Maddy asked, convinced she was about to learn some great secret that only doctors knew.

"You are," the doctor said.

Maddy considered that. She wasn't sure if he was being nice or rude.

"What do you mean?" she asked.

"Well, when I asked you if you would like to hear some French," the doctor said, "I asked it in French."

Maddy quickly thought back. Yes, the doctor had said, *"Est-ce que tu aimerais entendre un peu de Français?"* So that was French!

"In fact, everything I said from then on was also in French." The doctor smiled.

"Wow," said Maddy.

"And you answered in French also," he said, and went back to his chair, which puffed and wheezed as he sat down. Maddy thought that the doctor should lose some weight, but she also thought that a doctor would know that without having to be told by a nine-year-old girl. So she said nothing.

"Do you also speak Polish?" the doctor asked, and from the sound of the words, Maddy guessed this time he was speaking Polish.

She answered using the same kind of words. "I guess so, if this is it."

"Well, I never," the doctor said.

He pushed a button on a small metal box on his desk. It answered with his nurse's voice, although it sounded distant and tinny.

"Gabby, would you come in here for a moment please?" he said.

"Certainly, doctor," the voice said.

The door opened and the nurse entered.

"Yes, doctor," she said.

"Maddy, this is Mrs. Head," the doctor said. "Mrs.

Head, I seem to remember you telling me that you spoke Spanish."

"I learned it at school, and I practiced a little last year when we went on vacation to Majorca," she said.

"Would you mind practicing a little on Maddy?" the doctor asked.

"I'd be happy to," Mrs. Head said. "Does she speak Spanish?"

"I think we're about to find out," the doctor said.

Mrs. Head sat down on the chair next to Maddy, where her mom had been sitting.

Maddy thought Mrs. Head was pretty, with happy eyes, but used too much makeup.

"I am asking if speaking Spanish you thank you please," Mrs. Head said.

Maddy laughed.

"Did you understand her?" the doctor asked.

"A little," Maddy said.

"Interesting," the doctor said. "Mrs. Head, would you please try again?"

"Speaking the Spanish difficulty without language motor car," Mrs. Head said confidently.

"How about that time?" the doctor asked Maddy.

"No, sorry, I couldn't understand her," Maddy said.

"Thank you, Mrs. Head," the doctor said.

She rose and went back to her office.

"Japanese, French, Polish, but not Spanish," he muttered, making some notes in Maddy's file. "Now that is very interesting."

"Actually, I think I do speak Spanish," Maddy said after the door to the office had shut.

"You do? I thought you said you didn't."

"What I said was I couldn't understand Mrs. Head," Maddy said. "I think I speak Spanish, but I don't really think that she does."

The doctor chuckled and made some changes to his notes in the file.

"What are we going to do with you?" he asked.

Maddy didn't know the answer to that question.

Just then, the door opened, and Maddy's mom stood in the doorway. She did not look pleased.

"How are these tests going?" she asked.

"Very well," the doctor said. "You have a very charming and talented daughter."

"Humph," Maddy's mom said, which wasn't a word in any language that Maddy could understand, but her mom always seemed to say it when she was annoyed and didn't know what else to say.

"But it's not only Japanese that she speaks," the doctor said.

"She speaks another language?"

"A lot. In fact, so far I haven't managed to find a language that she doesn't speak."

"That's not right, is it?" Maddy's mom said. "Can you do something about it?"

"To be honest, I don't think there's a problem to solve," the doctor said. "A talent like this could be very valuable."

"No. It's not natural. It's not . . ." She seemed to catch her breath. "Valuable?"

"I mean, in a useful kind of way," the doctor said, but Maddy's mom didn't seem to have heard him.

"Valuable?" she said again.

"No, I simply meant . . ." the doctor began, but Maddy's mom walked over and took Maddy's hand, pulling her up out of the chair.

"Thank you, doctor," she said. "How much for today?"

"Uh . . . please see Mrs. Head on the way out," the doctor said. He was frowning.

Maddy caught his eye and winked at him to let him know that everything would be all right. He broke into a grin and shook his head.

"What an extraordinary young lady," he said.

CHAPTER TWO

An Invisible Friend

IF NOT FOR MADDY'S MOM, that might have been the end of that, and Maddy might never have gone on a dark and dangerous adventure.

Maddy's mom was a tall, thin lady with high, sharp cheekbones and bouffant red hair that took hours of blowing and brushing and huffing and puffing in the morning to keep that way. Her name was Gertrude. It was a rather old-fashioned name that had been handed down for generations in her family, but it had somehow skipped Maddy (for which she was grateful).

Maddy hadn't skipped the red hair, however. Unlike her mom's, though, Maddy's was a jungle of thick red springlike curls — and no amount of huffing and puffing or brushing seemed to make any difference. She had also inherited her mother's rather fierce temper, although

Maddy tried to keep that under control. Sometimes Maddy felt like there was a wild animal caged inside her, and she had to be careful not to let it escape.

When they got home from the doctor's, her mom disappeared into her bedroom and shut the door. Maddy could hear her talking on the phone, but she knew that when her mom shut the door, it meant she didn't want to be disturbed.

"Not unless there's a fire!" her mom had once said, quite abruptly, when Maddy had interrupted her to ask her something.

What that really meant, Maddy knew, was: *Not unless it's super important!* And there was nothing important, so she knew she should leave her mom alone for a while.

Instead, she climbed up onto the desk in her bedroom, opened the window, and crawled out onto the fire escape.

It was metal and cold and always left a crisscross pattern on the palms of Maddy's hands and her knees, which Kazuki called "alien skin."

She ran along the fire escape, being careful not to look down. You could see through the metal grille all the way to the ground below, and it was a very long way down. When Kazuki came to visit her, he never used the fire escape because he was afraid of heights. He always took the elevator down to her floor and knocked on the front door instead. But Maddy liked using the fire escape.

She tapped on the window of Kazuki's bedroom, where he was sitting, reading a book.

Kazuki, like Maddy, enjoyed reading books. Kazuki's books were written in a Japanese alphabet that went from the top to the bottom of the page and across from right to left, instead of left to right. Maddy found them hard to read because she kept going the wrong way.

Today she could see that he was reading an English vocabulary book. It was one of his books from school.

Kazuki's English was very poor, even though his family had moved to England over a year ago. His older brother Tsuji spoke good English, and Kazuki's teachers couldn't understand why Kazuki hadn't picked it up as well.

Maddy thought she knew. Tsuji was confident and outgoing and had made a lot of friends at school, so he was always speaking English. But Kazuki was quiet and shy and hadn't made any friends at all, so he didn't get to practice English that often.

Maddy tried to speak English to him, but it made for difficult and slow conversations so, as often as not, they would speak in Japanese.

"Hi, Maddy," Kazuki said (in Japanese).

"Open the window," she said (also in Japanese), and when he did, she climbed inside.

Kazuki was ten, and his room was covered with posters of things that made no sense to Maddy, like scary-looking Japanese men called samurai, with bald heads and long swords, and other men wearing black pajamas and black hoods that covered everything except their eyes. Those men had swords too and were called ninjas. When Kazuki grew up, he wanted to be a ninja warrior.

"Where did you go today?" Kazuki asked.

"To the doctor's," Maddy answered.

"Oh," Kazuki said. "Did he give you any medicine?"

"No," she said.

"Good," he said. "I hate medicine."

"Me too," said Maddy.

"My birthday present from Uncle Kiyoshi arrived today," he said.

It had been Kazuki's birthday the day before. Maddy had made him a colorful birthday card, and his parents had given him a new catcher's mitt and a baseball.

"What did your uncle give you?" Maddy asked.

"A ninja suit!" Kazuki said. "It's really cool. It's black and it has lots of secret pockets."

"Cool!" said Maddy.

"And it can make me go invisible," Kazuki said.

"That's exciting," Maddy said. "Invisible! Really?"

"Yes!" Kazuki said. "And no one can see me, and I can do anything I want."

"That's amazing," Maddy said, trying not to sound too skeptical.

"Yes, and when I am invisible, Mom can't see me at all. Today I sneaked a cookie out of the jar while she was in the kitchen, and she never saw anything."

Maddy thought that Kazuki's mom's cookies were terrible and tasted like seaweed, but she was too polite to say so, either to Kazuki or to his mom.

"You have to show me," Maddy said.

The ninja suit was all black. Black pants, a black tunic, and a black belt. Attached to the back of the tunic was a black hood that could be pulled down over his face like a mask. Only Kazuki's eyes and hands were visible when he put it all on. Then he put on some black gloves and that just left his eyes.

"Okay, now I'm going to go invisible," he said. Behind the face mask, Kazuki's eyes closed, and his brow furrowed in concentration.

He opened his eyes with a look of anticipation. "There!" he said. "Can you tell where my voice is coming from?"

"From your mouth, silly," Maddy said. "I can still see you as plain as flour."

"Oh." Kazuki looked disappointed. "Perhaps I did it wrong."

He shut his eyes and concentrated even harder, then opened his eyes and said, "Where am I now?"

"Right there," Maddy said, pointing at him.

"It's not working," Kazuki said. He looked like he was about to cry.

"Wait," she said. "Let me turn around, and you go invisible when I'm not watching."

"Yeah!" Kazuki said. "That's got to be it."

Maddy turned around and counted to three, then turned back.

Kazuki was gone.

"I can't see you," she gasped.

"I told you!" Kazuki said.

He was standing in the corner of the room. He had moved so quietly that Maddy hadn't heard him. He was standing so still in a shadow that at first she hadn't been able to see him until she had looked right at him.

It wasn't really invisibility, she thought, but it was quite extraordinary all the same.

"That's fantastic," she said.

"Now I can be a real ninja," Kazuki said, pulling his hood back.

Maddy looked around at the ninjas on the posters on Kazuki's wall. Maddy thought that to be a ninja warrior you would have to be strong and fierce and brave, but Kazuki was more quiet and gentle. Maddy couldn't imagine Kazuki as a fierce ninja warrior.

"And I'll be able to sneak right into Tsuji's room and play tricks on him," Kazuki was saying.

Maddy laughed. Tsuji was older and bigger than Kazuki and often picked on him. "That sounds scary."

"But when I have my ninja suit on, I won't be afraid," Kazuki said.

Maddy nodded.

"You're lucky that you don't have an older brother," Kazuki said.

"I guess," Maddy said.

"How come you don't have any brothers or sisters?" Kazuki asked.

"I'm not sure," Maddy said. "I asked Mom and she said

it was because they couldn't afford any more kids. She said I was very expensive."

Kazuki laughed. "When you say it like that, it sounds like she bought you in a shop."

Maddy laughed too. "I guess your mom and dad could afford to buy more kids than my mom and dad," she said.

"I guess so," Kazuki said. "Or maybe you were just really expensive because you can speak lots of languages."

"I don't know about that," said Maddy. "She's not happy about it."

"I think it's just because she doesn't understand," Kazuki said. "People are afraid of what they don't know."

"I suppose," said Maddy, and she gave Kazuki a small hug because she knew he was really talking about himself.

CHAPTER THREE

THE MAN FROM CHANNEL FOUR

THE MAN FROM CHANNEL FOUR came around on a Wednesday afternoon after school. Maddy was baking.

She was making muffins — the easy kind that came in a packet, and all you had to do was add a little water and spoon the mixture into a muffin tray and put it in the oven for a while.

Her dad, who was a chef and worked in a fancy restaurant, had shown her how to do it. Maddy's mom, on the other hand, didn't like baking and thought it was messy and unnecessary when you could buy perfectly good cakes and cookies at the supermarket, and fresh muffins and pastries at the bakery on the corner.

Maddy had just taken the muffins out of the oven and tipped them onto a cooling rack when the doorbell rang.

She didn't hear her mom going to answer it, so when

the doorbell rang a second time, Maddy went to the front door. There were smears of chocolate mixture all over her apron, on her face, and even in her hair (she was a rather messy cook), but she wasn't worried about that.

On the doorstep she found a rather floppy kind of man with long, fluffy hair and a wrinkly shirt, which was not very well tucked in. He peered at Maddy over the top of a pair of thick black glasses.

"Hello," said Maddy.

"Uh, yes, uh," the man said, which wasn't saying anything really. "You must be, uh, little Maddy. Is your, uh, mother or father home?"

She was about to answer him when she heard her mom's voice behind her.

"Hello, you must be Darcy," her mom said.

Maddy turned and looked at her mom. She had put her best dress and makeup on and had a gushy look on her face like when she met that singer from Scotland, or that actor who had once been on that TV show she liked.

But this man didn't look like an actor or a singer.

"Uh, yes, yes, that's me," the man said.

Maddy thought he said "uh" and "yes" too much.

"Come in," her mom said, pushing Maddy to one side. "Would you like a cup of tea?"

Maddy was about to go back to the kitchen, but her mom said, "Maddy, darling, would you like to join us for a muffin? I have some lemonade, too, if you'd like some."

"You're a very good girl to help your mom with the baking," the man at the doorway said.

Maddy just smiled.

They sat in the front room, which her mom always called the parlor, although it was also the living room and also the TV room, and when her parents had a dinner party it was also the dining room. But today it was just the parlor.

"Uh," the floppy man said after he had stuffed his mouth with not one but two of Maddy's muffins. "These are delicious. Delicious."

There were lots of crumbs on his jacket and a few in his pocket, which might come in handy if he got hungry later.

"Oh, it's nothing," her mom said with a wave of her hand.

Maddy just smiled again.

The man put his plate down and leaned toward Maddy. "Yes, well. What a pleasure it is to meet you, young lady. A pleasure indeed."

Maddy chewed slowly. Her mom had given her only

half a muffin, and it wasn't even the big half, so she was taking her time and making it last as long as possible.

"To meet me?" she asked after she had swallowed.

"Uh, yes, your mother invited us to talk to you."

Maddy was confused about why he said "us" when there was only one of him, and it must have shown on her face, because the man said, "I must apologize. My name is Darcy Holdem. I'm a researcher for *Smart Talk*."

"What's that?" Maddy asked.

"It's a television program."

"Really?" Maddy said.

"Yes, yes, yes. We've heard about your rather special abilities, and we're considering having you on our, uh, our show."

"On television?" Maddy asked, barely able to contain her excitement.

"Yes, on television," Mr. Holdem said. "Would you like that?"

"Yes! I've always wanted to be on TV!" Maddy said. "What would I have to do?"

On some television shows they had people doing all sorts of crazy things, like being marooned on a desert island, or running over slippery shapes and falling into swimming pools. On one Saturday morning kids' show, the guests were "slimed" by icky green goo that fell from the ceiling.

"We just want to talk to you about your ability to speak other languages," Mr. Holdem said.

Maddy looked at him suspiciously. "Will I get slimed?"

Mr. Holdem laughed. His bow tie quivered, and his glasses slid down his nose. "Goodness gracious, no," he said, pushing his glasses back up. "We don't slime people on our show."

"Will I fall into a swimming pool?" Maddy asked.

"No, nothing like that," he said. "We just want to interview you."

"Well, I suppose it would be all right," Maddy said. "As long as it's okay with Mom."

She knew that she had to ask permission for anything like this, and her mom often didn't approve. But to Maddy's surprise, her mom said, "Yes, of course you can, darling. Would you like another muffin?"

Now Maddy was starting to get suspicious.

"That's settled then," Mr. Holdem said. "But first I need to ask you a few questions. Just to make sure everything is as it seems."

"Okay," Maddy said.

"I am going to read you some phrases in different

languages," Mr. Holdem said. "I want you to tell me what they mean."

"Okay," said Maddy again. This sounded like a fun game.

Mr. Holdem pulled some white cards out of his jacket pocket.

"Here's the first one," he said.

Her mom was watching her closely.

"De spin is onder de tafel," he said.

Maddy bent down, peering under the coffee table. "No there's not!" she said.

"Not what?" her mom asked.

"A spider under the table," Maddy said with a little laugh.

Mr. Holdem laughed. "I see you understood."

"Yes, I did," Maddy said. "What language was that?"

"That was Dutch," he said. "Didn't you know?"

"No, I've never heard it before," Maddy said.

"You've never heard it before," Mr. Holdem repeated her words slowly, almost as if he didn't believe her. He picked up another card and said, "My mother flew to the moon in a rocket ship shaped like a banana."

"I'm not sure," Maddy said.

"Not sure about what?" her mom asked.

"I think Mr. Holdem said that his mother flew to the moon in a rocket ship shaped like a banana," Maddy said. "But that doesn't make any sense."

"Maybe not," Mr. Holdem said, "but that is exactly what I said in Maori."

Another card. "I love to eat apples, but only while under water," he said, in Italian this time.

Maddy giggled and told him what he had said. He made a note on that card and tried another.

"The eating habits of the South African anteater leave a lot to be desired."

Maddy translated that too.

"That was Croatian," Mr. Holdem said. He looked at Maddy's mom. "Well, I'm satisfied," he said. "Very satisfied. I'll be in touch about the dates and times, and will give you some details about where to go. Now, about the compensation we discussed."

"We can talk about that later," her mom said quickly.

"Uh, yes. Indeed," Mr. Holdem said.

"Thank you, Mr. Holdem," Maddy said. "I enjoyed playing your game."

Mr. Holdem beamed. "You are very charming. Charming," he said. "I look forward to meeting you again soon."

CHAPTER FOUR

TSUJI

AFTER MR. HOLDEM LEFT, Maddy went to find Kazuki to share her exciting news. He wasn't at home, but she found him out in the alleyway, playing baseball by himself.

The alley was a narrow, cobblestoned street that ran along the back of their apartment block and the backs of the houses on the next street. It was too narrow for cars.

Kazuki was throwing his new baseball against the wall at the end of the lane, catching it in his new mitt.

On the other side of the wall was a park, and Maddy could hear the shouts of the other kids in the neighborhood playing and laughing. They sounded like they were having fun, and it was quite sad that Kazuki was here by himself. Walls were not just made of concrete, she thought.

Kazuki's eyes brightened when he saw Maddy. "Hi, Maddy," he said.

"I'm going to be on TV!" Maddy blurted out, then told him all about Mr. Holdem and *Smart Talk*.

Kazuki seemed as excited as if it was him, not Maddy, who was going to be on TV.

"You want to play catch?" Kazuki asked when Maddy finished telling him her news.

She nodded. To be honest, Maddy didn't really want to because Kazuki was so good at it and she wasn't. But she knew he wanted to, so she always said yes.

Kazuki tossed the mitt across to her, and she backed away a little down the lane. "Ready?" he asked.

"Ready," she said.

Kazuki lined up in a pitcher's stance, drew back his arm, and let the ball fly. He had pitched for his little league team in Japan and was very good at it. All Maddy had to do was to keep her mitt in the one place and the ball would fly in a straight line right into her palm. She used her other hand to steady the mitt, and it was just as well that she did, because the ball hit the mitt so hard that if she had been using only one hand, she would probably have smacked herself in the face with the back of it.

She rolled the ball back to Kazuki because she wasn't very good at throwing. Often a ball would go off in strange and unexpected directions if she tried to throw it.

It skipped and bounced over the cobblestones.

Kazuki threw it again, just as hard, just as straight, and she rolled it back to him a second time. He was about to throw it again when a doorway about halfway down the alley bounced open, and Tsuji came out.

Tsuji liked picking on Kazuki and always said that it was just for fun, but Maddy thought that most of the time he was just being mean.

They were as different as chalk and cheese, Kazuki and Tsuji, and not because Kazuki was shy and Tsuji wasn't. Kazuki was small for his age and slight of build. Tsuji was tall and chunky. Kazuki was kind-hearted and generous. Tsuji was, well, Tsuji.

Kazuki stopped throwing the ball and held it.

"Hello, Maddy," Tsuji said.

"Hello, Tsuji," said Maddy, carefully.

"Hi, ugly," Tsuji said to Kazuki, who ignored him. Tsuji noticed the baseball. "Are you guys playing catch?"

Neither Kazuki nor Maddy said anything.

"Great! I love playing catch," he said. "Throw one to me." He advanced down the alley until he was in front of Maddy. "Come on, throw one to me."

Kazuki looked at Maddy and frowned. He knew exactly what Tsuji was up to.

"What are you, stupid as well as ugly?" Tsuji asked.

"You're the ugly one," Kazuki said.

"You're so ugly your doctor is a vet," said Tsuji.

"You're so ugly you make onions cry," Kazuki said.

"Yeah, well, you're so ugly . . ."

This carried on for quite a few minutes until Maddy got sick of it and cried, "Stop it!"

"So throw me the ball," Tsuji said.

Kazuki lowered his eyes, sighed, then reluctantly drew his arm back again and let the ball fly. It went a bit sideways, off target. He had done that deliberately, Maddy realized, trying to keep the ball away from Tsuji. But it didn't work. Tsuji stretched out an arm and nabbed the ball out of midair as it flew past. He didn't even need a mitt.

"Thanks," he said. "I needed a new baseball."

He turned and started to walk back down the lane.

Maddy blocked his way, and when he tried to push past her, she moved back in front of him. "Get out of my way, little girl," he said.

"Give me Kazuki's ball," Maddy said. "You know it was his birthday present." Inside, Maddy felt her temper start to stir.

"It's my ball now," Tsuji said. "He gave it to me. And it's not even my birthday." He laughed out loud at his joke.

"Give it to me," Maddy said and politely added, "please."

"Why? Is it your birthday?" Tsuji asked, laughing again.

"No."

"Then . . . no," Tsuji said. "Get out of my way."

He tried to push past, but she moved so he couldn't.

Her temper was rising like a wild animal starting to pace inside its cage. "Don't make me angry," Maddy said. "You wouldn't like me when I'm angry."

"I said no," Tsuji said.

"Even I don't like me when I'm angry," warned Maddy.

He opened his mouth to say something else but then looked at her eyes. Somewhere deep inside them he must have seen that wild animal peering back at him.

He looked at the ball, still shiny, bright, and new. He sniffed — a long, gurgling sound. Then from somewhere deep in his throat he hacked up a big glob of mucus, a huge yellow-brown thing that quivered and bubbled as though it was alive. He spat it onto the ball then tossed the ball into the gutter where it rolled, smearing the mucus into a long streak, collecting dust and old dry leaves.

"It's all yours," he said.

He pushed past Maddy and went back in through the door from which he had come out.

Kazuki walked over and looked at his baseball.

Maddy kneeled down. "Don't!" Kazuki said, but she did anyway. She picked up the ball gingerly and carried it over to a faucet on the wall by the entrance. She rinsed off the muddy slime and leaves and handed it back to Kazuki. He took it but looked as though he no longer wanted it.

"Tsuji's a bully," he said. "You're so brave to stand up to him."

"Not really," Maddy said.

"Well, I think you're brave," Kazuki said.

Maddy shrugged but said nothing.

She felt sorry for Kazuki. It was bad enough that he had no friends and was struggling to fit in in a country where everyone spoke a different language, without having to put up with a mean big brother as well.

But she also felt sorry for Tsuji. It couldn't be nice to be a bully. She felt a bit sad that he didn't know how to be a different kind of person.

"I'll tell you what I am nervous about," Maddy said.

"What?"

"Going on television," Maddy said.

"That's going to be so cool!" Kazuki said, brightening, the ball and his bully of a brother forgotten for now.

CHAPTER FIVE

SMART TALK

THE STUDIO WAS FULL of bright lights that hurt Maddy's eyes, but the producer lady told her not to squint or she'd look "sneaky." Maddy didn't want to look sneaky for her first time on television. The producer was a young Chinese lady named Ms. Yee, but she said Maddy could call her Jacquie.

It was exciting being on television. She got to sit in a big red chair with silver arms. It twirled in a circle when she pushed herself around with her feet . . . until Jacquie nicely asked her to stop doing it so the camera people could set their "focus."

The camera people had huge television cameras on stands that rolled across the floor and went up and down and around. It looked like an important job to be a cameraperson.

After a while, the interviewer, whose name was Devron Chapman, came and sat in another red chair next to s and chatted with her about the weather and her and other stuff that didn't seem to matter at all. thought he was trying to make her relax, but she her relaxed already, although she would have liked her chair again.

vron leaned forward and whispered to her. "Okay, it one more time."

ıddy giggled and pushed off with her feet, spinning etely around and coming back to face Devron with smile on her face.

cquie was looking in their direction, but Maddy saw on give her a wink, and that meant everything was

n the other side of Devron was a long sofa, and three people came to sit on it. Maddy wasn't sure who they were and thought maybe they were the next guests to be interviewed after her.

The first was a thin, ratty-looking man with pale skin and long hair on one side that he brushed over the top of his head to hide a shiny bald spot. Maddy thought it looked a little silly. He wore an old brown jacket with leather patches at the elbows, and there was an egg stain on his tie.

The next man was the most beautiful man Maddy had ever seen in her life. He was completely bald and his skin was dark. He had soft oval eyes and a huge smile that shined like the moon. A makeup lady came and patted down the top of his head with a powdered sponge as Maddy watched.

The third person was a lady, quite old, with kindly, wise eyes, and her hair was tied back in a long ponytail.

Maddy wondered what they were going to be interviewed about and was surprised when she found out it was her.

After some kind of finger countdown from Jacquie, Devron began to talk. He introduced himself and the show and then turned to Maddy. She thought she was probably supposed to be nervous but couldn't help herself from beaming with excitement.

"Hello, Maddy," Devron said.

"Hello, Mr. Chapman," Maddy said, as if she was just meeting him and hadn't been chatting with him for the last ten minutes.

"You can call me Devron," Devron said.

"And you can call me Maddy," Maddy said, forgetting that he already had.

There was laughter from the studio audience and

another smile from the beautiful man in the middle of the sofa.

Then she remembered about the green slime and, despite what Darcy the researcher had said, she looked upward to make sure there wasn't a bucket of slime suspended over her head.

"Everything all right?" Devron asked.

"Yes, thank you," Maddy said. "I was checking to make sure I wasn't going to get slimed."

Everybody roared with laughter.

It took Devron a moment to get his breath back so he could continue, but when he did, he said, "Maddy, it's lovely to have you here today. I think it's going to be a surprise for our audience. They have no idea why we are interviewing you today."

Maddy just smiled, not sure if he expected her to say something.

"Firstly, tell us a little bit about yourself, Maddy," Devron said. "What kind of things do you like to do?"

"Well," Maddy said, thinking hard about the question, "I like singing and dancing and cooking, and when I grow up I want to be on TV. Just like you."

"That's nice," Devron said.

"Not like you, exactly. I mean, not that I wouldn't want

to be like you, but I want to sing and dance, or maybe do cooking, not just talk to people." She began to get a little flustered. "Not that there's anything wrong with that."

"Let's start again," Devron said. "When I welcomed you, perhaps I should have said *konichiwa*, or *hej*, or *ciao*, or *kia-ora*."

Maddy smiled again.

"Did you understand what I said?" Devron asked.

"Yes, you said hello — lots of times," she said and added, "Once is usually enough."

More laughter.

Devron turned to the camera and said, "And now you see why this remarkable young lady is joining us today. Some people are fluent in two languages, others have mastered three or four. Me — some days I struggle with just one." More laughter from the audience. "But this young lady tells us that not only can she speak English, German, French, Spanish, and Japanese. In fact, she can speak any language."

In *fact*, Maddy had said nothing of the sort and rather suspected it was her mom who had told them that.

Devron said, "We've invited Maddy along today to see if it's really true that she is omnilingual or whether she is just a child prodigy who has managed to learn a lot of languages at a very young age. Today, our other guests in the studio are Magnus Sigmarsson, professor of Icelandic languages at the University of Reykjavík."

The audience clapped, and the thin, pale man with the ratty face nodded his head, which made his hair flop around. He smoothed it back with a hand.

"South Africa-born William Buthelezi, a native speaker of the Zulu language."

More applause as the man dazzled the audience with his huge smile.

"And Annie Whitehorse from New Mexico, USA, who speaks fluent Navajo."

The lady bowed her head graciously.

"I can tell you," Devron said, "that Maddy had no idea that these three people would be here today, nor did she know what languages they speak. This is the first time she has heard this, so she couldn't have had a chance to prepare for them."

He glanced at Maddy to see her reaction, and she gave him another big smile.

He continued. "First up, Professor Sigmarsson. Icelandic is regarded as possibly the hardest language in the world to learn. Perhaps you could ask Maddy a few questions and see how much she can understand."

The professor nodded his head, smiled a rather gritty smile, and turned to Maddy.

"Hello, young lady," he said, in what Maddy knew must be Icelandic. "You probably don't realize how hard it is to learn Icelandic. Few people, apart from those who were born there, can ever really understand the idioms. Do you understand any of what I have just said?"

He had spoken very quickly, running the words together almost as if he wanted to make it hard for her, Maddy thought.

She replied in the same language. "Mostly, but I don't understand what an 'idiom' is. Could you please explain that part?"

The professor was smiling at the audience, convinced he had outsmarted Maddy.

He said, "Of course. It's the . . ."

He stopped, suddenly realizing that she had asked her question in Icelandic. His eyes widened, and he seemed to go a little paler than before.

Devron smiled at Maddy, then turned to the camera. "That sounded convincing to me," he said. "However, my knowledge of Icelandic is pretty much nonexistent. Professor Sigmarsson, how did young Maddy do?"

The professor ignored Devron.

"Young girl, where are you from?" he asked in Icelandic.

"I'm English, actually," Maddy replied. "I live near Cambridge. But I'd love to visit Iceland one day. It sounds a bit cold though. Is it?"

The professor looked straight at Maddy with a harsh expression then looked at the studio audience. "She's a fraud," he said.

Maddy gasped.

There was a moment's silence.

"A fraud?" Devron asked, giving Maddy a sideways glance. "Why do you say that, professor?"

"It's a clever trick," the professor said, "but you can't fool me with such trickery. I am a professor of the Icelandic language. I know all the regional variations. Of course this girl can speak Icelandic — she *is* Icelandic! I can even tell by her accent the name of the town where she was born, Bolungarvík, which just so happens to be the same town in which I was born."

He folded his arms and leaned back on the sofa, quite satisfied with himself.

"Is this true?" Devron asked, a little nervously. "Were you born in Iceland, Maddy?"

"No," Maddy said. "I was born right here." She thought about that for a second, then she smiled at the audience.

"Actually, I think my mom bought me in a shop at the Main Street Mall."

The audience laughed again.

"She bought you? In the Main Street Mall?" Devron asked.

"I think so," Maddy said with a straight face. "That's where she usually goes shopping."

Devron was struggling not to laugh. He took another deep breath and continued. "But have you ever lived in Iceland?"

"Never," Maddy said.

"She's not telling the truth," Professor Sigmarsson said.

The audience went quiet. Devron, too, not sure what to say next.

Maddy clamped her lips together. She didn't like to be called a liar, and especially not on national television.

"So, in your opinion, Maddy is a native Icelandic speaker," Devron said.

"It's not an opinion — it is a fact," Professor Sigmarsson said.

"No, it's *not* a fact," Maddy said. "It's not even right."

"Do be quiet, little girl," Professor Sigmarsson said. He turned to Devron. "My time is valuable, and if I find out that your program is in on this, and that it's just a hoax or some kind of practical joke, then I will be very disappointed."

Maddy was breathing slowly in and out, trying to calm down.

"Professor, I can assure you that we have no knowledge of any practical joke or hoax," Devron said.

"I'm telling the truth," Maddy said, quite calmly, although she really wanted to jump up and shout it out loud.

If the professor had known Maddy better, he might have had an inkling of what was about to happen, and he would have probably stopped talking at that point. But he didn't. Instead, he smiled at Maddy in a most condescending way.

"Little Maddy," he began.

"No," Maddy erupted. "That's enough! I am not lying, and there's no need to be so rude. I could have said something about you spilling food on your tie or the funny way you brushed your hair, but I didn't. That's because I'm not rude like you."

She paused for breath, and in that breath, she suddenly remembered the cameras and the studio audience. She stopped, her mouth agape, and looked around.

Devron seemed frozen in place. Jacquie, the producer,

was running around in the background, whispering into her headset microphone. Professor Sigmarsson looked stunned.

Then someone, somewhere in the audience, slowly began to clap. A few others joined in, and it got faster and faster until the entire audience exploded with thunderous applause.

Professor Sigmarsson sat back in his chair and turned his head away with a miffed expression.

When the applause had died down, William Buthelezi said, "Might I be permitted to have a little word with the girl?"

"Of course," Devron said with a look of relief.

"Maddy, it is a great pleasure to meet you," William said. "And I'll tell you a secret. I, too, like to sing and dance."

Maddy liked William immediately.

He continued. "It would give me even greater pleasure to know that you can understand what I am saying."

It was a strange language, full of tongue clicks and whistles, and when Maddy tried to answer, she had to try a couple of times to get the sounds right.

"It is a pleasure to meet you as well," she said. "You have the biggest, nicest smile I have ever seen in my life."

William roared with laughter while Devron and the rest of the people in the studio all looked confused.

William turned to Devron and said, "She says she likes my smile. She most definitely was not born in Iceland. From her Zulu accent, I would say she grew up in Umzimkulu, where I'm from in South Africa. But I rather suspect that she is telling the truth. Perhaps not the Main Street Mall, though — more like a boutique shop on High Street."

Everybody laughed. To Maddy, he said in the strange clicking language, "You are a true wonder, my charming young friend."

Maddy turned red but beamed back at him.

Annie Whitehorse, the Native American woman, took her turn to ask a few questions in Navajo, and Maddy answered them too.

Maddy was quite enjoying the whole thing, although it was clear that Professor Sigmarsson was far from convinced and couldn't be persuaded that she was anything but a fraud — a fraud who had really grown up in Bolungarvík and was trying to fool him.

Afterward, as they were leaving the television station, Maddy and her mother met William Buthelezi again in the lobby.

He took her mom's hand and said lots of lovely things about Maddy. When they turned to leave, he presented Maddy with his business card.

"If I can ever be of service to you, please call me," he said. "I would be honored to be of assistance."

Maddy clutched the card as they went into the elevator.

The last thing she saw as the elevator doors closed was William's huge, shining smile.

CHAPTER SIX

THE OLD MAN ON THE TRAIN

THEY HAD TO WAIT a long time for the train that went back to Maddy's house. When it finally arrived, it wasn't very full, and they had a whole compartment to themselves. Maddy and her mom sat silently. Maddy was tired from all the talking she had done in the television studio. Her mom was holding an envelope the producer had given her after the show was finished. She had a strange expression on her face, and she glanced at Maddy frequently.

Maddy looked out the window at the countryside as it went by. There were lots of hedges and fields with cows and sheep.

Ahead, the track started to curve, and she could see the train cars in front of theirs. She watched the front part of the train as it curled around the track and disappeared into a hole in the side of the mountain. A tunnel! Tunnels were exciting, she always thought. When you were in a tunnel, you were actually inside a mountain, even if only for a short time.

Her mom's eyelids began to droop, and she rested her head back against the seat cushion and drifted off to sleep. Maddy also felt tired and struggled to keep her eyes open.

Closer and closer the tunnel came, and then everything went black except for the light from the ceiling. All the light bulbs seemed to be broken, apart from the one above her head. The bulb was so bright and everything else around her was so dark that she couldn't see anyone or anything — not even her mom. That was frightening even for someone who wasn't afraid of the dark.

Then, out of the shadows in front of her came a voice. The sound startled her. It came from the man who was sitting on the other side of the compartment. Strange that she hadn't noticed him when they had first sat down. His voice was low, like Reverend Pritchard's at church, but even deeper, and it rumbled like a train going across a bridge. He spoke in English, but with an unfamiliar, thick accent.

"Hello, Maddy," the man said. "I saw you on television." As he said it, he leaned forward into the cone of light that was shining down on Maddy.

He was very old, she noticed. Reverend Pritchard was

old — he was at least seventy — but this man was much, much older than that. His hands were gnarled, knotted by age and maybe by arthritis. He wore quite raggedy clothes.

Maddy didn't feel alarmed, though. He had a comforting manner, a little like the doctor, and she felt quite warm and cozy just to be sitting near him. It was an odd sensation, but Maddy knew that some people were like that. Other people made you feel cold and prickly and you wanted to move as far away from them as possible.

"You are a very, very clever girl," the old man said.

"Why, thank you," said Maddy.

"What you can do is very special," he said.

"The doctor said it was extraordinary," Maddy said, and wondered as she said it why she was telling these things to a stranger.

"Quite. In fact, I haven't met anyone who could do that since . . ."

He leaned back, and his voice disappeared with him into the darkness. There was silence for a moment, and then he moved into the light again.

"I think you have a touch of the magic about you," he said.

"I like magic," Maddy said. "I once saw a magician at the school fair. He made cards disappear, and rabbits and scarves appear, and . . ." She became excited as she recalled this and told the old man all the things that the magician had done.

He listened patiently and smiled a lot, but when she had finished, he said, "He sounds very clever, Maddy, but that man was a conjurer, not a magician. He did tricks, not magic."

"Do you mean *real* magic?" Maddy asked with her mouth and eyes open wide. There was no such thing according to her dad, who was usually right about these things.

The man looked gravely at her. "In days long gone, before schools and books and television and the Internet, there was a lot more magic in the world," he said. "Then scientists came along and changed everything." His eyes dropped to the floor for a moment, then lifted back to Maddy.

"It wasn't all bad," he continued, "because without scientists we wouldn't have cell phones and coffee machines and satellites and nonstick frying pans. But scientists decided that everything had to be explained by their rules and anything that couldn't be explained by science simply didn't exist. There was no room for unicorns and fairies and magic in this new world."

"Is there really magic in the world?" Maddy asked, her heart pumping.

"Just a little left, I think," he said. "And I think a little is in you."

"I can't do magic," Maddy said. "I'm just an ordinary girl."

"Oh, you're far from ordinary," he said. "You're very far from ordinary. But listen to me carefully."

He stared right at her, and Maddy found she was transfixed by the bottomless pools of darkest blue in the center of his eyes. "There are many types of magic in this world. Most of it is small magic, but beautiful magic."

"Yes?" Maddy said breathlessly.

"But there is also a darker magic. The magic of deep, hidden places. Of things which cannot be spoken of. Beware of the black magic."

Maddy listened, transfixed.

The old man got up, very slowly, and moved toward the door. He was unsteady and, Maddy thought, not very well.

"I think this is my stop," he said. "I have to go now."

He paused and peered out at her from under long white bushy eyebrows. "I'll do what I can to watch out for you."

That seemed a strange thing to say, and Maddy was

about to ask him what he meant, but suddenly the train left the tunnel, which had been much, much longer than Maddy remembered from when they went through it the other way. She didn't think a tunnel could be longer one way than the other, but it certainly seemed like it.

The compartment filled with light, which made her blink. When she finished blinking, the old man was gone. The train began to slow down, which meant they were approaching a station . . . the old man's station, Maddy supposed.

Her mom was just waking up.

"He was really nice," Maddy said.

"Who was?" her mom asked.

"That old man who was just here," Maddy said.

Her mom looked around, confused. "You shouldn't talk to strangers," she said.

She was right, Maddy knew, but the old man hadn't seemed like a stranger.

"He saw me on TV," Maddy said. "He thought I was very clever."

"Don't be silly," her mom said. "Today they were only recording the show. It doesn't go on TV until next week."

"Oh," Maddy said. "Perhaps he was in the audience then."

The only problem was, she hadn't seen him in the audience, and she thought she would have noticed him if he had been there.

"Don't talk to strangers," her mom said again.

CHAPTER SEVEN

PROFESSOR COATELOCH

MADDY HAD ANOTHER VISITOR the next week. It was unusual because Maddy hardly ever had visitors. Her mom and dad often had visitors but not Maddy. (Unless you counted Kazuki, and she didn't, since he only lived next door.)

But Mr. Holdem had come to visit her, and now Professor Coateloch had come to see her too. It was exciting to have so many visitors.

Both her mom and dad were there because it was a Tuesday and the restaurant where her dad worked was closed that day.

Maddy was busy reading a cookbook after school when the professor arrived, so she didn't go out to see who was there until her dad came to her door. He filled the whole doorway.

Her dad was a big man, very tall, and quite roly-poly.

Never trust a thin chef, he always said. He was wearing an old T-shirt and a baseball cap, which were his usual clothes when he wasn't working.

He smiled when he saw that Maddy was reading a cookbook.

"There's someone here to see you," he said.

"Really? Who is it?" Maddy asked.

"A professor from the University of Cambridge," her dad said. "Professor Coateloch."

Professor Coateloch did not look anything like what Maddy had expected. She thought a professor should have a long, gray beard, and wear black robes, and be quite old. But Professor Coateloch was not wearing black robes and did not have a long, gray beard. She would have looked rather funny if she did, Maddy thought, because Professor Coateloch was a woman. She wore a pretty apricot-colored dress and had her black hair pulled back in a ponytail.

"Hello, Maddy," she said.

"Hello, um, Professor," Maddy said.

"Professor Coateloch needs your help," her dad said and laughed as though that was funny. He often laughed at things that weren't really funny. He just liked to laugh. But Maddy didn't mind. She loved his big jolly laugh.

"What kind of help?" Maddy asked.

"Maddy, it seems that you have quite a special ability," Professor Coateloch said. "I won't pretend to understand it, and while there are a number of my colleagues in the linguistics department who would like to study you, that's not what I'm here for."

Maddy waited for her to continue.

"This is quite a long story," Professor Coateloch said.

Maddy smiled at her. "I like stories," she said. "Especially long ones."

Her dad laughed at that, and Professor Coateloch laughed too.

"Maddy, there are hundreds of different languages in the world today," Professor Coateloch said. "But if we look back in history, there were hundreds more that have died out because people stopped speaking them. In ancient Rome they spoke Latin, but nobody speaks that language anymore unless they study it at school or in college."

"Do you think I could speak that language, too?" Maddy asked.

"Let's find out," the professor said. She continued in a different language. "Right now I am talking to you in Latin. Do you understand me?"

"Yes," Maddy said.

"Good girl," Professor Coateloch said in English.

"Some languages have completely disappeared. And many languages don't even use the same alphabet that we use in English."

"Like Japanese," Maddy said.

"That's right," Professor Coateloch said. "And in the olden days there were many other alphabets."

"Tell her about the monks," Maddy's dad said, and winked at Maddy.

"Certainly," the professor said. "There is an ancient monastery in Bulgaria. That's a country in Europe near Greece and Turkey. The monastery is on an island in the Black Sea. Do you know where that is?"

"No, not really," Maddy said.

"Never mind," Professor Coateloch said. "Bulgaria is one of the oldest countries in the world, and this monastery was built thousands of years ago."

"Wow," Maddy said. She was trying to imagine anything that old.

"Yes, wow," Professor Coateloch said. "In the monastery there is a very old book. Well, not a book like you would know it. It is a series of scrolls."

"What's a scroll?" Maddy asked.

"It's like a roll of paper," Professor Coateloch said. "Except it's not really paper — it's made from animal skin. It's called parchment. These scrolls were written in an ancient language that has been lost for over a thousand years. Nobody knows how to read this book. The alphabet is a very early form of Cyrillic — that's the type of letters that people in that part of the world use. It's called the Glagolitic alphabet. Here's what it looks like."

She took a piece of paper from her briefcase and put it on the coffee table. Professor Coateloch was right. It certainly didn't look like the alphabet Maddy learned in school, or Kazuki's Japanese books either. It looked like funny squiggles drawn by a small child. She could tell it was a type of writing, though, from the way the letters were grouped into words.

Professor Coateloch said, "The scrolls were only discovered a few years ago, and since that time, linguists have been trying to translate them, but so far, nobody has managed to."

"Why are they so interested in them?" Maddy asked.

"These scrolls are very special," the professor said. "There are no others like them in the whole world. The monks who look after them believe they contain secret knowledge."

"That is exciting," Maddy said. "Do you have a copy of them?"

Professor Coateloch shook her head. "Nobody does," she said. "The monks will not allow them to be copied or photographed."

"That's just silly." Maddy's dad laughed.

"It's what they believe," Professor Coateloch said. "Maddy, we were hoping that you might be able to help us translate the scrolls."

"I don't think I can read those kinds of letters," Maddy said.

"Would you try?" the professor asked. She pointed to the piece of paper. "This is a different language but from the same part of the world, and around the same time. This one is called Proto-Slavic. It is an excerpt from the Bible. Does it make any sense at all to you?"

The professor hesitated before handing Maddy the paper. Maddy sensed that this was an important moment for her.

Maddy felt quite excited by the whole thing and just a little bit nervous, but her dad winked at her, and the nervousness went away.

She stared at the piece of paper, intrigued but confused by the strange yet neat characters. Some of the words were long and others were short, but none made any sense to her. Not even a single character made sense.

She shook her head. "Sorry." She handed the paper back to the professor. "Wait!"

Just as she was passing it back, out of the corner of her eye, it suddenly seemed to come into focus.

"What?" the professor asked.

Maddy said nothing and put the paper down on the table in front of her, not really looking at it, but looking past it. When she did that, the words seemed to make sense. Slowly, she shifted her gaze across the table until she was staring right at it, and this time she could read it as clearly as if it was English.

"Many have undertaken to draw up an account of the things that have been fulfilled among us, just as they were handed down to us by those who from the first were eyewitnesses and servants of the word." Maddy grinned a big mouth full of teeth and clapped her hands. "I did it!" she squeaked.

"That is incredible." The professor shook her head. Her voice was soft. "Maddy you are truly amazing. Nobody has spoken that language for hundreds of years, yet you were able to translate it."

"The child is a genius!" her dad said, and laughed again.

"I'd love to help," Maddy said.

"Wonderful," Professor Coateloch said. "But there's

one problem. You see, we can't bring the scrolls to you, so we would have to take you to the scrolls."

"Where are they again?" Maddy asked.

"Bulgaria," Professor Coateloch said.

Maddy sat there with her mouth open, and her eyes blinking. She had never been out of England before. And Bulgaria sounded a very long way away.

"Bulgaria?" her mom said. "Nobody said anything about Bulgaria!"

"It's a lovely country," the professor said. "And the town we would be visiting, Sozopol, is on the shores of the Black Sea. You could visit the beach or go sightseeing while Maddy and I work on the scrolls."

"It's a long way to go." Maddy's mother sniffed.

"There must be some other way," her dad said.

Professor Coateloch shook her head. "If you want to read the scrolls, you have to go to the monastery."

"In Bulgaria." Her mom screwed up her face.

"What do you think, Maddy?" the professor asked.

"I'd love to go!" Maddy said. "But . . ." She looked at her mother.

"To Bulgaria? Not me," her mom said. "You know I'm afraid of flying. Besides, there would be lots of people speaking strange foreign languages. I wouldn't understand a word they were saying."

"It has to be you, dear," her dad said. "You know that I can't afford to take time off work at the moment."

"Certainly not," her mom said. "I couldn't possibly."

"Sozopol really is a beautiful seaside town," Professor Coateloch said.

Maddy's mom crossed her arms and said nothing.

"I'd love to go, but I can't," her dad said.

There was a long, awkward silence.

"Would you be willing to let me accompany Maddy?" Professor Coateloch said at last. "I mean, we'd have to sign some papers, awarding me temporary guardianship or some such arrangement, but I can promise you that I would look after her as if she was my own daughter."

"Oh, I don't know," Maddy's dad said.

"I am not sure we want our daughter traipsing all over the world with a total stranger," her mom said.

"Not that you're a stranger," her dad said. "Not now."

Her mom leaned over and whispered in her dad's ear. He looked a little uncomfortable. She nudged him.

"Of course, if you were to reconsider the amount of the . . . uh . . . compensation," he said.

"If that will help," the professor said doubtfully. "I'll talk to my colleagues and see if we can adjust the offer."

"When would this trip be?" Maddy's mom asked. "Maddy can't take time off school, you know."

"Of course not," Professor Coateloch said. "When is the next school vacation?"

"In just two weeks!" Maddy said.

"Perhaps then," the professor said. "I'll talk to my colleagues tomorrow about the . . . financial side of things."

"These scrolls," Maddy asked, "do they have a name?"

"Yes, we think so," Professor Coateloch said. "Here it is in the old language."

She pulled a piece of paper from her briefcase and put it down in front of Maddy. On it were hand-drawn characters that were similar to, but not the same as, the other ones. Maddy glanced at them and then away a couple of times until they began to come into focus.

"Can you understand that?" Maddy's dad asked.

"Yes, I can," Maddy said, a worried look coming over her face.

The three adults watched Maddy and waited.

"*The Paths of Ancient Magic*," Maddy said.

★★★

The next day, Maddy's mom took her to have her photograph taken, and the week after, a letter arrived in the mail addressed to Maddy. When she opened it, out fell a little burgundy book with the word "Passport" on the front cover.

CHAPTER EIGHT

PACKING

MADDY PACKED HER OWN BAG for the trip. She didn't have a suitcase, so she just emptied her schoolbag and put everything in that she thought she might need. She put in lots of pairs of socks and underwear, her best jeans, and the skirt she wore to church, along with some old shorts and T-shirts in case they had to do any exploring or anything exciting like that.

She also packed her swimsuit, because she had read about the Black Sea in a book in the school library and found out that it was a very popular place for tourists, with lovely warm water. So maybe there would be time for a swim. Even with all of that, her backpack was only half full.

Kazuki arrived while she was packing.

"When do you leave?" he asked.

"On Saturday," she said.

"Are you excited?" he asked.

"Actually, I'm very nervous," Maddy said.

"Why?" Kazuki asked.

Maddy stopped packing and sat down on her bed. She had been thinking about the old man on the train and what he had said. When she remembered it now, it didn't seem real. The compartment had been empty when they sat down, she was sure of it, and the tunnel couldn't have taken that long to get through, and he couldn't possibly have seen her on TV, so none of it made sense.

Perhaps she had fallen asleep on the train and dreamed the whole thing.

Or perhaps not.

"What's wrong?" Kazuki asked, sitting down beside Maddy.

"A few weeks ago I was on the train," she said. "I think I might have dozed off to sleep. Then I woke up, and there was an old man, and he told me to beware of black magic or something like that."

"Why?" Kazuki asked.

"I don't know. I thought it was just a dream, but then Professor Coateloch told me about the ancient scrolls, and now I don't know what to do."

"Do you believe in magic?" Kazuki asked.

"I'm not really sure. I don't think so," Maddy said.

"What are you going to do?" Kazuki asked.

Maddy took a deep breath. "I guess if I don't go, I'll never find out."

"Find out what?" Kazuki asked.

"Anything," Maddy said. There was a pause.

"Where are you going in Bulgaria?" Kazuki asked.

"First to the capital city, which is called Sofia," Maddy said. "Then we go by train to a city called Burgas and by bus to Sozopol. Then we take a boat over to the island where the monastery is."

"Wow. That's a lot of traveling," Kazuki said. "You might need a ninja to protect you." He made some cool karate moves with his arms.

Maddy smiled but then realized he was being serious. "That's very brave of you, Kazuki, but I'll be fine," she said.

"What about the black magic?" Kazuki asked.

"It was probably a dream," Maddy said, "in which case, there's nothing to be afraid of."

CHAPTER NINE

MR. SLAVINSKI AND HIS FUNNY MONKEY

THE AIRPORT WAS FULL OF PEOPLE: people of all different shapes, sizes, colors, and clothes. Maddy had never seen so many people all in one place before. There was a whole team of teenagers bouncing a soccer ball around between them. There were men in long robes and other men wearing colorful floral wraparound skirts. There were people with pins through their noses and their ears. People with tattoos on their arms and on their faces.

Two teenage goth girls seemed to be watching Maddy as she walked with Professor Coateloch through the airport. They wore black leather jackets, and their hair was dyed jet-black. They had black nail polish and black eye makeup and black lipstick.

A man with long hair and a bushy beard was sitting on one of the seats. He was the biggest man Maddy had ever seen in her life, and quite possibly the biggest man in the world. He was taller sitting down than most people were standing up. He sat on the end of one of the rows of seats, and the arms of the chair seemed to have to bend to fit him in. The seat next to him was empty. Well, not entirely empty — on it sat a toy monkey wearing bright blue pants, a red waistcoat, and a hat. It was the kind of hat that men wore in old-fashioned movies. The monkey looked so real that Maddy thought it would start moving by itself. Then it did! It turned its head to look at her, and she realized that it *was* real. It was a little capuchin monkey like she had read about in books.

She stopped suddenly. Professor Coateloch stopped a few paces farther ahead when she realized that Maddy wasn't with her anymore.

Maddy stared at the monkey, and it stared back at her. She smiled, and the monkey smiled right back.

The big man had his eyes shut, but he opened one and regarded her for a moment before closing it again. Maddy thought he looked sad. Scary, but sad.

The monkey, however, was very happy to see Maddy and jumped up and down on the seat. It even did a backflip, landing right back on its feet. That was about all it could do, however, because of the thin leash attached to a collar around its neck that disappeared into the gigantic hand of the man.

"What's your name?" Maddy asked, but the monkey only made some little chirping noises.

The big man must have heard Maddy, but he didn't say anything, so after a few more seconds of making faces at the monkey and it making funny faces back at her, she caught up with Professor Coateloch, who was waiting patiently for her.

"What a funny monkey," Maddy said.

"I think he liked you," the professor said.

Kazuki and his mom were waiting for them at the departure gate to say goodbye. Kazuki had insisted on coming to see Maddy off. Maddy's dad was working, and her mom hadn't come because she didn't like airports, so Maddy was glad that Kazuki came.

All the other people seemed to have someone to say goodbye to them. There were lots of people hugging and crying and kissing.

But Maddy didn't hug Kazuki or cry, and she certainly didn't kiss him. She just said goodbye and Kazuki said, "Have a nice flight." Then they both waved, and Maddy and Professor Coateloch went through the gate that said, "Departures."

They stood in line at a place called "Customs" with all the other people who were flying out of the country that day. A friendly man in a blue jacket checked Maddy's brand-new passport, and it must have been all right because he let her through with a wink.

They went through a security check after that where a large X-ray machine looked inside Maddy's bag without even opening it, and she had to walk through a metal detector.

Then they walked past a lot of shops selling perfumes and electronics and finally into the gate area to wait for the airplane.

"That's her," a voice said in front of them, and Maddy looked up to see a security guard in a white shirt and black pants walking up to them with a lady in an airline uniform. "I saw her on television," the guard said.

The lady with him was a kind-looking lady with long brown hair and a name badge that said "Stephanie Day."

"Are you sure?" she asked the guard.

"Positive," the guard said.

Stephanie walked up to Professor Coateloch and said, "Excuse me, ma'am, are you this girl's mother?"

The professor shook her head. "No, just her guardian for a few days."

"Oh," Stephanie said. "Would it be okay if I spoke to her for a moment?"

"You'll have to ask her." Professor Coateloch smiled. "It's fine with me."

Stephanie kneeled down in front of Maddy and said, "Excuse me, is your name Maddy?"

"Yes," Maddy said.

"Tony here," she looked at the guard, "told me that you were on television and that you speak many languages. Is that true?"

"Which part?" Maddy said. "That I was on TV or that I speak lots of languages?"

"Oh, I mean . . ."

"It's okay." Maddy grinned. "Yes, both of those things are true."

"Good," Stephanie said. "Do you by any chance speak Bulgarian?"

"I don't know until I try," Maddy said. "But I expect I can."

Stephanie looked confused by that but smiled anyway. To Professor Coateloch she said, "Would it be all right if Maddy came with us for a few minutes?"

Professor Coateloch didn't look very happy and said, "Do we have time? We're boarding soon."

"We'll only be a few minutes," Stephanie said.

"Please, Professor Coateloch," Maddy said.

"I'll make sure she is back in plenty of time for boarding," Stephanie said.

"I'd better come too," the professor said, standing up.

"We have to go back out through security and customs," Stephanie said. "It's going to be difficult enough to get Maddy through. I promise I won't let her out of my sight."

The professor sat back down. She still didn't look happy, but she was probably just being protective, Maddy thought. She was responsible for Maddy on this trip.

Stephanie took Maddy's hand, and they walked back through the security area into the customs area.

As they walked, Stephanie explained. "We have a Bulgarian passenger who doesn't speak much English. We do have a Bulgarian translator, but we can't get through to him. We're trying to find somebody else at the moment, but Tony seemed convinced that you could help."

"I'll try," Maddy said.

They walked toward the customs counters.

The big man with the monkey was standing in front of one of the counters, the monkey perched on his shoulder, talking to the same customs man who had winked at Maddy. Two more security guards were standing around him, although their heads didn't even come up to the big man's shoulders. They both had hands held up toward the big man as if they were trying to stop traffic.

The big man was trying to explain something, but his English was very poor.

"Me. Me fly. You me fly. Yesterday, today," he said, waving a ticket in the air.

"Sir, I'm going to have to ask you to calm down," one of the guards said.

"Me fly. You me fly. Yesterday, today," the man said again. He was angry about something, Maddy could see, and that was making everybody else nervous.

"Excuse me, sir," Stephanie said to the man. "This young lady may be able to help."

"Mr. Chester fly," the man said.

Two police officers were approaching now from the other direction. Maddy thought that the man might end up in a lot of trouble if somebody didn't do something — and soon.

"Mr. Chester fly!" He was shouting now.

The guards were shouting at him too, but he wasn't listening to them. The whole customs area was in disarray with people moving and milling about everywhere. Some of the other customs officers were trying to process travelers but it was getting harder and harder with all the fuss.

"Excuse me," Maddy said.

The big man ignored her, or perhaps just didn't hear her with all the shouting going on.

She tried in French. *"Excusez-moi, monsieur."* Then in Polish, Spanish, Icelandic, Zulu, and even Navajo. Each time, he glanced at her briefly before roaring again with his few words of broken English. The monkey was jumping up and down on his shoulder, screeching.

Maddy didn't know how to speak to him because she didn't know what kind of words he used. As long as he kept trying to speak English, she couldn't help.

"No luck?" Stephanie asked, very nicely, as though it was her fault, not Maddy's.

"Can you ask him to say something in his own language?" Maddy said.

"I really don't know how," Stephanie said, looking up at the mountain of a man.

Maddy looked around at all the people. "Excuse me, would everybody please be quiet?" Maddy said.

Everybody ignored her, including the giant in front of her. They all kept shouting at each other.

"Excuse me," she said. Then louder, "Excuse me!"

But it was clear they were all far too busy to listen to a small girl.

"Please, everybody stop talking!" Maddy said much more loudly, starting to go quite red in the cheeks.

Still they ignored her.

"Everybody just shut up!" she yelled, feeling as though her hair was standing on end and steam was coming out of her ears.

When that had no effect, Maddy marched right up to the big man and before Stephanie could stop her, she kicked him in the shin as hard as she could.

The man stopped shouting and waving the ticket. The guards stopped shouting. The police officers stood still. Everybody went silent.

The big bearded man turned, and his deep-set eyes dropped lower and lower until they rested on Maddy. She shrank back. The man towered over her. The police officers stepped forward rather nervously.

Then a strange thing happened.

The big man sank slowly to his knees. Maddy had to take a couple of steps back to move out of his way. He sat on his haunches and frowned. Deep wrinkles like folded paper opened up across his forehead and around his eyes.

Then he began to cry.

His sobs were almost as big as he was. They welled up inside him and rippled up through his chest before bursting out through his nose and mouth.

Everybody stood there, and nobody did anything and nobody said anything — they all just let the big man cry, tears pouring down his face, splashing off like a miniature waterfall to the floor.

"I didn't think I kicked him that hard," Maddy said.

Stephanie shrugged. She seemed as confused as Maddy.

"Sorry," Maddy said, and although the man didn't understand her, the sobs shuddered to a halt.

He looked at her then asked in a voice that was so deep it must have come from the bottom of the ocean, "Why did you kick me?"

So that was Bulgarian, Maddy thought, listening to the sound of the words.

"I wanted to get your attention," she said, in the same language.

"You speak Bulgarian!" the man realized.

"I'm sorry if I hurt you," Maddy said. "I didn't mean to make you cry."

The big man looked at her for a long moment, then for no reason that Maddy could see, he began to laugh — a big belly laugh that shook his whole body.

"You didn't hurt me," he said. "A little flea like you, hurt Dimitar the Giant? That is a joke to tell my friends!"

"Then why did you cry?" Maddy asked.

Dimitar's face became sad again. "My father died a few days ago," he said. "I came here for the funeral."

"Oh," Maddy said, not sure what to say next. "Why did he die?"

"He died because he was very old," Dimitar said. "But I still miss him very much."

"I'm sorry," Maddy said. She reached out and hugged the big man to make him feel better. She had to stand up on his knees to do it, and even then she could only just reach up around his neck.

"Remarkable," Tony the guard said.

Maddy climbed back down off the big man's knees and stood in front of him.

"Do you know this man?" Stephanie asked.

"No. I just thought that he needed a hug," Maddy said. "His dad died."

"I can't believe I cried," Dimitar said. "That took me a bit by surprise. I didn't even cry at the funeral."

"Maybe you should have," Maddy said.

Maddy put out a hand and took one of his. Her fingers could barely wrap around his thumb, but still it made him smile a little bit. She thought she should introduce herself and said, "My name is Maddy West."

"I'm Dimitar Slavinski," Dimitar said.

"Dimitar the Giant," Maddy said.

"Ah, you've heard of me," the big man beamed.

"Not till a minute ago," Maddy said truthfully. "Is this your monkey?"

"No. Yes," Dimitar said. "It is the monkey of my father, but I suppose he is mine now. His name is Mr. Chester."

That made Maddy laugh, but she couldn't explain why.

"Why did your father have a monkey?" she asked.

"Because he was very old and sick," Dimitar said. "Mr. Chester is a trained monkey. He has been trained to do simple things like opening bottles and even dialing numbers on the telephone."

"Excuse me." It was Stephanie speaking. She kneeled beside Maddy. "Do you think you could explain some things to him for us?"

"Of course," Maddy said.

"He wants to take the monkey on the airplane," Stephanie said. "But we don't allow animals in the cabin. Some airlines do, but that is not our policy."

Maddy explained that to Dimitar, who held up a plane ticket. "But I bought him a ticket," he said.

"Even with a ticket, he can't go in the cabin," Stephanie said. "He has to go in the luggage compartment in a cage."

Maddy translated.

"He can go on the plane?" Dimitar said.

"Yes, in a cage," Maddy said. "Would that be okay?"

"I don't think he'll like it much," Dimitar said. "But it's better than nothing. Why didn't they tell me that before?"

"I think they were trying to," Maddy said.

Stephanie stood up and went to the customs counter where she started talking on a phone.

Mr. Chester leaped down off Dimitar's shoulder at that and landed on top of Maddy's head. "Mr. Chester!" Dimitar said.

"It's okay," Maddy said. "I think he's sweet."

Mr. Chester climbed down onto Maddy's shoulder and started rubbing his tiny fingers through her hair. "What's he doing?" Maddy asked, giggling.

"That means he likes you," Dimitar said. He got up off the floor and sat in a nearby chair, which groaned under his weight.

"I like him too," Maddy said. "And I'm very sorry for kicking you."

Dimitar smiled. "I think you probably did the right thing. What a wonderful girl you are."

Stephanie kneeled down again. "I have arranged a cage for the monkey," she said.

"Mr. Chester," Maddy said.

"Okay. They will be here in a few minutes, and then Mr. Chester will have to go to the cargo people."

Maddy told Dimitar that.

"Would you like to see a few of his tricks while we wait?" Dimitar asked.

"Do we have time to see some tricks?" Maddy asked Stephanie, who checked her watch then nodded.

First, Dimitar got Mr. Chester to sit down, which he did with his legs crossed and his arms folded, just like the younger kids at school. Next, he got Mr. Chester to do a backflip, then to salute.

"Watch this," Dimitar said.

He began to make beatbox drum sounds with his mouth. Mr. Chester started hip-hop dancing. He was breaking and locking and popping. He did the running man and the cabbage patch, and he even stood on his head and spun himself around.

Maddy laughed with delight, and before she could help herself, she found herself dancing along with him, copying his movements — except for standing on her head and spinning around!

DEPARTURES
LAX

When they had finished, everyone laughed and clapped.

"What a funny monkey!" Tony said.

"What a delightful girl," Stephanie said.

Then the man with the cage came, and it was time to say goodbye. Maddy was sad because she thought she would never see Dimitar or Mr. Chester again.

And then the strangest thing happened.

Mr. Chester reached inside Dimitar's jacket pocket and pulled out a piece of paper, which he handed to Maddy.

"Mr. Chester!" Maddy said. "You naughty monkey." She handed the paper back to Dimitar without looking at it. Dimitar took it, but his face had turned sad again. Mr. Chester jumped up and snatched it out of his hand and handed it back to Maddy. "Mr. Chester!" Maddy said again.

This time she looked at the paper, which was folded in half. At the top were the words "Funeral Service" and a name: "Aleksandar Boris Slavinski."

"It is the program for the funeral of my father," Dimitar said.

"Time to go," Stephanie said.

Maddy tried to hand the program back.

"It's all right," Dimitar said. "You take it."

"Maddy, you don't want to miss your flight," Stephanie said.

"Bye, Dimitar," Maddy said, tucking the program in a pocket and giving him a quick hug. "Bye, Mr. Chester." She held out her hand to the little monkey, who grabbed it in both of his hands and kissed it like an old-fashioned gentleman.

They went back through security and were walking down a long corridor toward the gate lounge when Maddy remembered the program and took it out, wondering why Mr. Chester had been so insistent that she have it. She unfolded it and got such a shock that she stopped walking.

"Are you all right, Maddy?" Stephanie asked, turning back.

Maddy looked at her with wide eyes. There was a picture of Dimitar's father on the front of the program. At first she thought she was imagining it. Then she thought she must be mistaken. But there was no doubt. The face in the photograph was too distinctive to be anyone else.

"Dimitar's father was the old man I met!" she exclaimed.

"What old man?" Stephanie asked.

"On the train!" Maddy said.

"What train?" Stephanie asked.

CHAPTER TEN

TWO SURPRISE VISITORS

THERE WAS A BIG ROAR from the engines, a whooshing sound, and Maddy was pressed right back in her seat as if by an invisible hand. The plane zoomed faster and faster down the runway, then up into the sky.

Maddy was in the window seat, and the professor was sitting by the aisle. In between them was an empty seat.

Maddy looked at the professor. "Are we really flying?" she asked.

"Yes, we are," the professor said.

Maddy looked out of the window at the streets and cars getting smaller and smaller below them.

"It's like magic," she said.

Professor Coateloch laughed. "It's not magic," she said. "It's science."

Maddy knew that, but it still seemed magical to her

to be up so high in the sky on their way to a completely different country.

That made her think again about the old man on the train: Dimitar's father. What a strange thing to happen. And then to meet Dimitar at the airport. It couldn't just be a coincidence . . . could it? It was too much to think about, so Maddy put it out of her mind and decided to think about it later when she wasn't so confused and flabbergasted by the whole thing.

She toyed with the funeral program, which was still in her pocket, neatly folded. She considered talking to the professor about it, but something made her hesitate. Dimitar's father had told her to be wary of magic, and suddenly Professor Coateloch had shown up asking Maddy to help her with the scrolls. She seemed nice, but it was still a strange coincidence. Maddy decided not to tell the professor for now. She could always talk to her about it later.

Below them, the streets and cars disappeared as the plane flew up through the clouds.

"Did there really used to be magic in the world?" Maddy asked.

"Many people think so," Professor Coateloch said.

"So is that what these scrolls are all about?" Maddy

asked, wondering if that might give her a clue about Dimitar's father and his strange warning.

"Well," Professor Coateloch hesitated, "it's a little bit complicated, Maddy."

"I'm quite clever with complicated stuff."

The professor laughed. "Indeed, you are. When the world discovered science, most people stopped believing in magic. It was easier to believe in science because you could prove science, but you couldn't prove magic."

That was strangely similar to what Dimitar's father had said on the train. A cold finger ran up and down her spine, and she shivered.

"Why not?" Maddy asked.

"Because there were so many tricksters pretending to do magic."

"Like conjurers?" Maddy asked.

"Yes, exactly."

"So if someone could do real magic, people just thought he was another trickster," Maddy said.

"That's right," Professor Coateloch said.

"So is the book real?" Maddy asked. "The scrolls? Are they honestly magic?"

"Oh, I doubt it," Professor Coateloch said. "But scientists like me want to study them anyway."

Maddy thought about that. It seemed funny to her that science had driven magic out of the world, but now it was scientists who wanted to find out about magic. She couldn't work out how to say what she was thinking, however, so she didn't.

"I'll be back in a moment," Professor Coateloch said. She undid her seat belt and walked toward the back of the plane where the toilets were.

Maddy stared back out the window. She couldn't see the ground anymore, only white fluffy clouds, like a bunch of cotton balls making a huge carpet that spread in every direction. She realized that they were flying higher than the clouds. It was the first time in her life she had ever seen clouds from the top instead of from the bottom.

When she turned back, Kazuki was sitting next to her, which gave her such a great shock that she squealed. Kazuki was wearing his ninja suit but was just taking off his mask.

"Kazuki!" she said. "What are you doing here?"

"I couldn't let you go off on such a big adventure all by yourself," Kazuki said.

"But, but . . ." was all Maddy could say.

"I said you might need a ninja to protect you," Kazuki said.

Maddy was about to say that Kazuki was not a real ninja but stopped herself because that might have hurt his feelings. It was very brave of him and not like him at all.

"Thank you, Kazuki," she said, and meant it.

"I won't let anything bad happen to you," Kazuki said. "I promise."

Maddy smiled. Kazuki wasn't very large, and he wasn't very strong. She thought if anything, it would be she who had to protect him, but she didn't say that. "How did you get on the plane?" she asked.

Kazuki looked at her and made a face like she had just said something stupid. "I went invisible," he said.

"And it worked?" Maddy said. "I mean . . ."

Kazuki laughed. "I didn't really go invisible. Well, sort of. I sneaked away from Mom and went to the customs area, but I wasn't sure what to do. I mean, I brought my passport, but I didn't have a ticket. I was going to try to go invisible, but then this huge man starting shouting and everyone was running everywhere, and in all the confusion I just slipped past the customs counters."

Kazuki seemed to have a real knack for not being seen, Maddy thought.

"That was Dimitar," she said. "I've got a strange story to tell you about him. But what about security?"

"They didn't ask me for a ticket," Kazuki said. "They just made me walk through the metal detector."

"But they must have checked your ticket when you got on the plane," Maddy said.

Kazuki shook his head. "I went through with a big family. The dad was holding all the tickets, and the lady was in a hurry and I think she must have miscounted."

Maddy shut her mouth once again. In a way, Kazuki had been invisible. If she could speak strange, ancient languages, then who was she to say whether or not Kazuki could do something amazing, too?

What she was most surprised about, though, was that Kazuki had gone through so much trouble. He was such a quiet and nervous boy and was the last person she could imagine doing anything like that — yet here he was!

"What's the strange story about the big man?" Kazuki asked.

Maddy opened her mouth to reply, but just then, Professor Coateloch arrived back at the seat.

"I'll tell you later," Maddy whispered.

The professor was even more surprised to see Kazuki than Maddy had been.

"Hello?" she said. "You're Maddy's friend, aren't you? You came to see us off at the airport."

"Yes, Kazuki decided to come with us," Maddy said.

"Where are your parents sitting?" the professor asked.

Kazuki just smiled at her.

"He doesn't speak much English," Maddy explained, then translated the question for Kazuki.

"They didn't come — only me," Kazuki said.

"And they didn't mind?" the professor was clearly quite confused.

Kazuki shook his head.

Professor Coateloch sat down, staring at Kazuki with her eyebrows furrowed.

After a while, an attendant brought them meals.

"Professor Coateloch," Maddy asked after the meal, "how many languages do you speak?"

"Just three," the professor said. "English, French, and Latin."

"Three languages. That's very impressive," Maddy said.

"Nowhere near as impressive as you," the professor said.

"Are there other people who can speak lots of languages?" Maddy asked.

"There are many people who are fluent in five or six languages," she said. "And I know someone who can speak nineteen languages. I did hear of a man in Brazil who claimed he could speak more than fifty languages, but I don't know if that was ever proven."

Maddy translated all that for Kazuki.

Professor Coateloch said, "President James Garfield of the United States could write in Latin with one hand and Ancient Greek with the other hand at the same time!"

"Wow!" said Maddy.

Toward the end of the flight, the flight attendant who had served them their drinks came back with a man in a uniform.

"Ms. Coateloch?" the attendant asked.

"Yes," the professor said.

"And this is Maddy, who is traveling with you?" The attendant smiled at Maddy.

"Yes," the professor said.

"Are you the pilot?" Maddy asked the man.

"No, I'm the purser," he said. "I'm in charge of the cabin."

"And would this be Kazuki Takamori by any chance?" the flight attendant asked.

Professor Coateloch looked at Maddy.

Maddy nodded.

"Kazuki, can I see your passport?" the purser asked.

"He doesn't speak English," Professor Coateloch said.

Maddy translated for Kazuki, who reached inside his ninja suit and pulled out a passport from an inside pocket. The purser checked it, and then handed it back to him.

"Kazuki, your parents are very worried about you," the attendant said.

"He ran away from his mother at the airport," the purser said. "They've been searching everywhere for him."

Kazuki seemed upset as Maddy translated. "I left her a note," he said.

"That's how we found out you were on the plane," the attendant said. "But they are still very upset."

"Nobody could understand how you managed to get past customs and security," the purser said.

"I thought he had changed seats to sit next to Maddy," Professor Coateloch said.

"Well, there's nothing we can do right now," the purser said. He looked sternly at Kazuki. "But don't go anywhere."

Maddy smiled at that. Where was there to go?

Then the purser said, "The police in Bulgaria have been notified, and they'll be at the airport to meet the plane."

"Is Kazuki in trouble?" Maddy asked.

"I don't think so," the attendant said. "The police just want to get him back home safely to his parents."

The attendant and the purser went back to doing other important plane stuff.

Maddy put her arm around Kazuki's shoulders. She felt sorry for him. He had done something brave, and it had all gone wrong. But she couldn't help feeling a little relieved. Now she wouldn't have to be responsible for him.

But even as she thought it, she felt guilty for thinking it.

Kazuki began to cry.

CHAPTER ELEVEN

SOFIA

THEY LANDED IN SOFIA, the capital city of Bulgaria. Maddy, Professor Coateloch, and Kazuki were asked to leave the plane first, while all the other passengers stayed in their seats.

Two police officers — one male, one female, both wearing crisp blue shirts with dark ties and peaked hats — were waiting at the end of the jetway.

Maddy expected them to be stern with Kazuki, but it was quite the opposite. The male officer gave Kazuki a big, friendly smile, and the female officer kneeled down in front of him and began to talk.

Maddy translated as the officer explained that although Kazuki had broken the law, he wasn't going to be in any trouble. His parents just wanted him home as soon as possible. A lady from the Japanese Embassy was coming to the airport to help sort out the arrangements, and they were going to book him a seat on the next available flight back to England.

Kazuki glanced back at Maddy as he was led away, and she was surprised by the look in his eyes. He no longer looked as though he was going to cry. If anything, she thought, he had made his mind up about something.

After Kazuki and the police officers left, Maddy and Professor Coateloch were allowed to go and collect their bags.

The baggage collection area was crowded. Maddy saw Dimitar standing in a line of people moving slowly toward an exit. He had a small suitcase slung over his shoulder. She waved, but he didn't see her. He was probably in a hurry to collect his monkey from the luggage handlers, she decided. That was a shame. She would have liked to ask him about his father.

Maddy's backpack and Professor Coateloch's suitcase were going around on a large black conveyor belt with all the other passengers' luggage. The professor went to get a cart to put their bags on. Maddy's backpack came past, and she picked it up. It seemed heavier than before. She was just about to hoist it onto her shoulders when the backpack moved . . . all by itself.

Confused and alarmed, she prodded the backpack with her finger. It moved again.

Maddy looked around for the professor, not entirely sure what to do. After a moment's hesitation, she unzipped the backpack and pulled it open slightly. Two small eyes peered up at her from the shadows inside. She was so frightened by what she found that she almost dropped it.

She opened it wider. A tiny monkey was curled up on top of the sweater that she had packed in case it was cold in Bulgaria.

"Mr. Chester," she whispered. "What are you doing in there?"

Mr. Chester chirped quietly at her.

He must have escaped from the cage, she thought. He had such clever little hands that maybe he was able to reach through the bars and undo the lock. But why was he in her backpack? Had he known it was hers?

Regardless, Dimitar would be very upset when he got to the cargo place and found his monkey wasn't there. She looked around for him, but he was gone.

"What are we going to do with you?" she asked. "You're a very naughty little monkey."

Mr. Chester chirped again and grinned at her, which made her giggle.

Maddy saw the professor walking back toward them with a luggage cart.

"Here's Professor Coateloch," she said. "She'll know what to do."

Then a curious thing happened. Mr. Chester popped his head out of the top of Maddy's backpack and peeked at the professor walking toward them. He ducked back down into Maddy's backpack and raised one finger to his monkey lips.

"Here we go," Professor Coateloch said as she arrived.

Maddy looked back at Mr. Chester, who raised his finger once again to his lips and winked at her.

Maddy quickly shut the bag.

"Everything okay?" Professor Coateloch asked.

"Yes, everything's fine," said Maddy.

But inside, her mind was spinning and her heart was thumping — had she really seen what she thought she'd seen?

There were so many strange things happening that she wasn't quite sure what to believe. It seemed like Mr. Chester didn't want her to tell Professor Coateloch he was there. But if she couldn't tell the professor, whom could she tell?

Something very strange was going on. First, Dimitar's

father had turned up on Maddy's train talking about magic. Now his monkey had appeared in her backpack. And from what she had seen so far, this was no ordinary monkey. Maybe if she just looked after Mr. Chester for now, she could find a way to return him to Dimitar later.

She was still worrying about this when they arrived at the customs line. The last people from their flight were going through, and just after they arrived, another long line of people began to come in behind them, off another flight. They were lucky to have gotten in before the crowd.

The customs man was bald, but he had a long mustache. He smiled down at Maddy when she stepped up to the counter and handed over her passport. Professor Coateloch stepped up with her, but the man held up a hand and said, "One at time."

"But we're traveling together," the professor said.

"One at time," the man repeated.

Professor Coateloch moved back and stood behind a white line that was painted on the floor. The man turned to Maddy.

"Welcoming in Bulgaria," he said in rather poor English. "For why is the porpoise of your trip?"

"We are here to visit an old monastery," Maddy said in Bulgarian.

"You are Bulgarian?" The man looked puzzled and continued in Bulgarian. "But you have a British passport?"

"I'm English," Maddy said. "But I can speak Bulgarian."

"You must have had a good teacher," the man said. "Do you have anything to declare?"

"What does that mean?" Maddy asked.

"It means: do you have anything in your bag that you shouldn't have?"

"Oh no," Maddy said. "I'm only nine."

"I didn't think so," said the customs man. "So no food or animal products?"

"What are animal products?" Maddy asked.

"Anything that comes from animals," the man said. "Like meat or leather — things like that."

Maddy sighed. She should have told Professor Coateloch about the monkey. Now she was going to be in big trouble. But she couldn't lie. That would get her into even bigger trouble.

"Do animals count?" she asked, hoping the answer would be no.

But the man said, "Definitely. What kind of animal would you have in your bag, young lady?"

"A monkey," Maddy said.

The man laughed. "Toys don't count."

"He's a real monkey," Maddy said. "He can do tricks and everything."

"Of course," the man said with a smile.

"Do you want to see him?" Maddy asked.

The man looked past her at the long line of people waiting and shook his head.

"I'm sure it is a very nice monkey. I don't need to see it," he said.

Maddy breathed a sigh of relief, which made the man laugh.

He stamped something in Maddy's passport and waved her through. While she waited for the professor to come through, she opened the bag again to check on Mr. Chester. He was sitting up, and he gave her a worried look.

"It'll be all right, Mr. Chester," Maddy said. "I'll look after you until we find Dimitar. I promise."

Whatever was going on, Maddy was sure that it was something much bigger, much stranger, and much more mysterious than she could possibly imagine.

CHAPTER TWELVE

SOZOPOL

SO FAR BULGARIA had been a pleasant surprise. It was nothing like Maddy had expected. For some reason, she had imagined gloomy old castles and ancient stone buildings surrounded by cobblestone roads, full of the strange foreign people her mom had been worried about.

But it turned out to be a pleasant, modern country, and there was nothing gloomy about it. The skies were blue, and the countryside was green, and the people seemed nice. All in all it looked like a very happy place to be — and a lot less grimy and gloomy than many parts of the town where she herself lived.

From the airport they caught a train to Burgas, and from there, a bus to Sozopol.

At the train station in Burgas, Maddy had another surprise when she saw a large poster in a glass case.

It was for a wrestling match. She had seen wrestling posters back home in England, and this was like them, with two fierce men glaring at each other and a wrestling ring behind them. Above their heads was a belt made of leather and gold plaques, and she guessed that this was the prize they were fighting for. One of the men was a very muscly man with a bald head and narrow, stabbing eyes. The other man was Dimitar the Giant. Maddy stared at the poster.

So Dimitar was a wrestler — and a famous one, if this poster was any indication.

A minibus from the hotel picked them up from the bus station in Sozopol, and the driver told them lots of interesting stories and facts about the city as they drove through the streets.

Maddy drew in her breath when they came around a sweeping corner, and there before them was a sparkling expanse of blue. The sun was low in the sky behind them shining out over the sea. It was one of the most beautiful things Maddy had ever seen.

"That's the Black Sea," Professor Coateloch told her.

"But it's blue!" Maddy said.

"I know," the professor said.

"That's silly," Maddy said.

"South of here is another sea called the Red Sea," Professor Coateloch said. "And that's blue too."

"What were they thinking?" Maddy said.

Not far from the shore, she spotted an island: the large lump of green-covered rock made a hole in the glittering surface of the sea. The setting sun caught the island, making it glow like a beacon. Maddy pointed to it, and the professor nodded. That was the island they were going to visit.

As she watched, it seemed to shimmer on the surface of the water, like a mirage, like some place that wasn't actually real but existed only in your imagination.

Maddy felt herself drawn to the island, pulled toward it by a gentle hand, and yet . . . and yet at the same time, there was something dark about the island, something about the way it faded in and out with the tricks of the light from the setting sun — something a little unsettling.

She was no longer sure if she wanted to visit the island at all. No longer sure if the gentle urging that drew her in that direction was the attraction of something warm and wonderful, or something bad . . . like a spider luring prey into its web.

Those were silly thoughts, she knew. She thought it must just her imagination playing tricks on her because she was tired from all the traveling.

***

The hotel was in the old part of the town. All the houses and buildings looked like they had been there for hundreds of years.

Near the hotel they passed a house with a miniature windmill at the front, the sails turning slowly in a light breeze. Below it was an old-fashioned cart with big wooden wheels. It made Maddy think of times long ago and what life must have been like in those days. Before science and technology, cell phones, and nonstick frying pans, like Dimitar's father had said.

The driver took them right to the front door of the hotel and double-parked in the narrow street, then unloaded Professor Coateloch's suitcase from the back of the minibus.

Maddy had not let go of her backpack for a moment. It had been on her knee the whole way. She hadn't wanted Mr. Chester to get bounced around in the luggage compartment.

"This is where we'll be staying," Professor Coateloch

said. "It's too late to go to the island tonight, so we'll get a good night's sleep and catch the boat out in the morning."

Maddy had no objections to that. She was quite tired, and she could see that it was going to be dark before too long. She decided she would rather face whatever was waiting for her on the island in the bright light of day.

A concierge in a red uniform showed them to their room. Maddy and the professor each had their own bedroom with a lounge in between them. In the lounge were two sofas and a tiny refrigerator that was full of chocolate bars and granola bars and soft drinks and beer and tiny bottles of wine.

"Mom wanted me to call her when we got to Sozopol," Maddy said after she had put her backpack safely in her bedroom.

"Okay, certainly," the professor said, nodding her head. "But it will be a very expensive call on a hotel phone. How about we get a phone card in the morning? That way it will be almost free."

"That sounds like a good idea," Maddy said.

The professor ordered some sandwiches for dinner. They were chicken with salad in between thick, crunchy slices of brown bread, and they were delicious.

Right after dinner, Maddy asked if she could go to

bed and the professor nodded. "Of course. You must be exhausted."

But Maddy really just wanted to let Mr. Chester out of the backpack before he pooped all over her clothes.

She shut her door first, in case the professor walked past, and then opened her backpack. Mr. Chester looked up at her. He had taken off his hat and was wearing a pair of Maddy's underwear on his head.

"Mr. Chester!" Maddy whispered so Professor Coateloch couldn't hear. "You naughty monkey!" She snatched her underwear away.

Mr. Chester grinned up at her, then put his hat back on, hopped out of the backpack, and sat up on the bed, looking at her expectantly.

With a quick glance at the door, Maddy brought out a sandwich quarter that she had wrapped in a napkin, hiding it in her pocket during dinner.

Mr. Chester tore chunks off the bread and ate it quickly, but he didn't touch the chicken or the salad.

"Eat your greens," Maddy said, but Mr. Chester ignored her and started exploring the room instead.

He ran up one of the curtains by the window and walked along the curtain rod at the top. He disappeared under the bed for a moment and reemerged chewing on something he had found under there.

"Eww," Maddy said.

Maddy watched in amazement as Mr. Chester climbed up things and down things using his hands and feet (which were just like little hands) and his tail to climb, hang, and swing all around the room. She guessed that he was using up some energy after being cooped up in the bag for so long, and she didn't blame him. But he was so quick and so boisterous, a little monkey whirlwind, that he began to knock things over. Maddy ran around after him, trying to catch things before they could crash to the floor. It was all she could do to keep up with him.

"Stop it, Mr. Chester," she whispered, but he paid her no attention. "Stop it, or the professor will come in to see what all the noise is about!"

After a few minutes, he began to get tired of his monkey gym and sat down next to Maddy on the bed. She went around the room straightening things up and putting them back where they belonged. On the nightstand, Mr. Chester found the remote for the TV and turned it on.

"Clever boy!" Maddy said. He must have been trained to do that for Dimitar's dad.

Mr. Chester flipped through all the channels. He didn't seem interested in any of the cartoons or the other kids' shows that Maddy would have liked, and when he found a nature channel with a documentary about African animals, he covered his eyes with one hand while he quickly changed stations.

He eventually settled on a cooking show where the presenter was showing how to make a cold soup called *tarator.*

Maddy thought that her dad would have been interested in the show, although he didn't speak Bulgarian, of course, so he wouldn't have understood a word of it. She was surprised that Mr. Chester was interested in cooking, but he seemed to be watching and listening with great interest, so she left him to it.

She was lying on the bed, not really watching the TV, when there was a small sound from Mr. Chester, and a moment later a strong smell wafted up from that direction.

"Mr. Chester, did you fart?" Maddy asked.

Mr. Chester gave her a grin, and saluted like a soldier on a parade ground.

"Yuck! That stinks!" Maddy said. Maybe he was a little bit magic, and maybe he wasn't, but whatever he was, he was still a monkey.

Just then there were two short taps on the door, and Professor Coateloch asked, "May I come in?"

Mr. Chester scrambled under one of the pillows on the bed and lay very still as Maddy said, "Yes, of course."

Professor Coateloch popped her head around the door, and said, "I'm off to bed myself. I was just checking to make sure you were okay and to see if you needed anything."

"I'm fine, thank you," Maddy said.

"Good night," said the professor.

"Sweet dreams," Maddy said, and the professor closed the door.

Mr. Chester crawled out from under the pillow.

Maddy found that she was getting quite tired so she turned off the TV and the light.

Mr. Chester immediately turned the TV back on.

"No, Mr. Chester," she whispered. "It's bedtime." She turned the TV off again and put the remote under her pillow so he couldn't turn it on again.

"Good night, Mr. Chester," she said.

He took off his hat and laid it on the nightstand, then took off his jacket and folded it neatly, placing it next to the hat. Then he leaned over and gave Maddy a quick peck on the cheek.

"Eww!" Maddy said. "Monkey kiss!" But she didn't mind, really.

Mr. Chester curled up into a tight ball on the pillow next to her head and shut his eyes.

"Good night, Mr. Chester," Maddy said again in a slow, tired voice. "No more farting."

He didn't move, and Maddy snuggled down into the bed and drifted off to sleep.

After a while, her breathing settled into a regular rhythm, with just the occasional little snore. The only light in the room came from the moon, which shined brightly through the thin gauze curtains over the windows.

In that gentle glow, anyone watching would have seen that Mr. Chester wasn't really asleep at all. As soon as he was sure that Maddy was asleep, he propped himself up on the pillow and gazed around the room. He kept watch with eyes that were far too wise for a little capuchin monkey.

It was as if he, and he alone, had some idea of the terrors that the next day would bring.

CHAPTER THIRTEEN

GOING HOME

IN THE MORNING, MADDY found herself wondering how Kazuki was doing. She bet his parents were angry with him, but maybe they also would be so relieved to have him back safely that they wouldn't be too angry.

Professor Coateloch ordered a light breakfast of toast and cereal, and they ate it together. The professor kept looking out the window at the island, barely visible through a light mist across the water. She seemed excited and even a little nervous.

"The island doesn't look very far away," said Maddy.

"No, we're close now," the professor said. "Very close."

She seemed fidgety.

After breakfast, they got dressed in their hiking clothes. The professor took two water bottles from the fridge and put them in a small daypack. Then they went down to reception, where a lady in a brightly colored dress was seated behind the desk.

"I'd like to book tickets on the boat to the island," the professor said.

"Professor Coateloch?" the lady asked.

"That's right," the professor said.

"There's someone here to see you," the lady said.

A police officer rose out of a comfortable armchair in the lobby. He had clearly been waiting for them. His uniform was immaculate with sharp creases at the corners of his dark trousers but none at all in his shirt. His collar and tie were precise. His uniform hat was in his hand, and his hair was neatly combed with a part in the center. He put his hat on as he walked over to them.

"I am Inspector Teodorov of the National Police Service," he said in good, but accented English. "It has taken us a while to track you down."

He extended a hand, which the professor shook warily as if she was worried he might bite.

"I need to ask you if you have any knowledge of the whereabouts of Kazuki Takamori."

"Kazuki!" Maddy said. "What do you mean?"

"I thought he had been sent back to England," the professor said.

The inspector looked grim. "Unfortunately not. Kazuki disappeared while our officers were trying to sort out his return flight. No one has seen him since."

Maddy gasped.

"Why didn't anyone let us know?" the professor asked.

"As I said," Inspector Teodorov continued, "we have been trying to locate you. So have Maddy's parents."

The professor looked uncomfortable. "We had to change hotels," she said. "There was a mistake with our booking. I was going to call Maddy's parents this morning with the new details."

Maddy hadn't known any of that, but she was much more concerned about her friend, lost and alone in another new country where he didn't speak any of the language. "Poor Kazuki!" she said.

"His parents are flying over as we speak," Inspector Teodorov said. "Believe me, we are doing everything we can to find him before they get here."

"That might not be easy," Maddy said.

"Why is that?" Inspector Teodorov asked.

Maddy noticed the professor looking at her closely.

"He's very good at not being seen if he doesn't want to be," Maddy said. "It's almost like he's invisible."

The policeman smiled briefly, creasing the lines at the

corners of his eyes. "Well, in any case, your parents want you home, I'm afraid. They've asked if you can return home immediately."

"Yes, of course," Maddy said. "But . . ."

"But what?" the inspector asked.

"But we've come such a long way," Maddy said. "To see the scrolls."

Inspector Teodorov looked at the professor, who nodded. "I've brought Maddy to visit the old monastery. Might we be permitted to do that before we leave?"

The inspector shook his head. "If it was up to me, yes. But I have strict instructions from my commander. He has been getting phone calls from the British Embassy. The disappearance of this boy has been somewhat of an embarrassment to us."

"I understand," the professor said. "But we are here now. So close. So very close."

"I'm sorry," the inspector said.

Professor Coateloch does not seem to be taking this news very well, Maddy thought. Her face was starting to get red, and her voice began to rise like Maddy's did when she lost her temper.

"Young man," she said, "I have been waiting years for the opportunity to read these scrolls. Scrolls that nobody has read in hundreds — maybe thousands — of years. This may be our only chance to find out what they say. I am sure you can bend the rules." She had pulled herself up to her full height. Maddy hadn't realized until that moment just how tall she was. She was a good head taller than the inspector and she stared down at him with narrowed eyes.

He seemed unperturbed. "Madam, I cannot change my orders."

Now the professor's face was bright red, and there was a fire in her eyes, which were mere slits. She started to argue some more, but then she caught Maddy's gaze. She shut her mouth and also her eyes, and when she reopened them, they were calmer. "Of course," she said. "Of course. We must do what we are told."

"As must we all," Inspector Teodorov said. "I will give you a ride to the Burgas train station. Colleagues of mine will meet you in Sofia and escort you to the airport.

"I hope Kazuki is all right," Maddy said.

"We'll do our best to find him and get him home safely," the inspector said.

The inspector waited in the reception area while they went back to their room and packed their bags. It didn't take long.

Maddy went to use the toilet before the long ride and

when she came out, the professor was hanging up the phone.

"I tried to get through to the British Embassy," she said a little too quickly. "To see if they could persuade the police to change their minds. But no luck."

Maddy had a strange feeling that the professor was lying.

***

Sitting in the back of the police car, Maddy felt sad and worried. She was worried about Kazuki. What had happened to him?

And she was worried about Mr. Chester. What was she going to do with him? She couldn't take him back to England on the plane.

She was sad for the professor who had been so excited about maybe being the first person to read the scrolls in hundreds of years. They had come on such a long journey, by plane, train, and bus, only to miss out on the very thing they had come here for.

At the train station in Burgas, they made a little pile of their luggage in front of a seat, and Maddy sat down while the professor and the inspector went over to the ticket window. Maddy opened her backpack to check on

Mr. Chester. He looked snug and sound, and he winked at her. What was she going to do with him?

The train station was crowded. It was much busier than when they had arrived the night before. There were people everywhere, scurrying in different directions. Maddy was looking around, watching all the different types of people, wondering where they were all off to in such a hurry. Then she saw a strange thing. Two girls dressed all in black with black hair and black makeup. Two goth girls. One taller than the other. Maddy was quite sure they were the same two girls she had seen at the airport in London.

And they were walking straight toward Maddy as if they knew her. Now that they were closer, Maddy could see them more clearly. They both had black hair pulled back into long braids. The smaller one had lots of pimples, including a huge one in the middle of her forehead. She had a tight, pinched mouth and a constant frown. The other — a big, awkward, and gangly girl — had bright blue eyes and looked nervous.

"There you are!" the spotty one said loudly in Bulgarian. "Mother has been looking everywhere for you!"

"Me?" Maddy said. "I don't think . . ."

"Mother has been looking everywhere," repeated the big girl.

"I don't even know you," Maddy said.

"Come on, or we're going to be late," Spotty said. She grabbed Maddy's arm and pulled her up off the seat, picking up Maddy's backpack in her other hand.

"But . . . but . . ."

"Mother is going to be really angry," the big girl said, seizing Maddy's other arm.

Maddy looked around for the professor and the inspector, but they seemed to have disappeared. They weren't in the line by the ticket window anymore.

"Why do you always have to run away?" Spotty said in the same loud voice.

"Yeah, you always run away," the big girl said.

That was when Maddy figured out why the girls were talking so loudly. They wanted the other passengers and staff at the train station to hear. They wanted everyone to think that Maddy was just a naughty little girl who had run away from her family. But that wasn't true.

It could only mean one thing — she was being kidnapped! Maddy gasped with fright and then found her voice. "Help, help!" she cried.

"Oh, stop it, Maddy," Spotty said. "Don't play those silly games again."

"Don't play your silly games, Maddy," the big girl said.

These girls knew her name!

Maddy tried to sit down and make the girl drag her across the floor, but that didn't work. The big girl just picked her up and put her over her shoulder like a sack of potatoes and carried her toward the escalators that led up to the street.

"Help, I'm being kidnapped!" Maddy shouted. A woman on the escalator going down next to them frowned at her as she descended toward them.

"Help me!" Maddy said, staring right at the woman.

"Stop it, Maddy," Spotty said loudly. "You know what trouble you got into last time you said silly stuff like that."

The woman on the down escalator looked away as she passed.

"Help me!" Maddy yelled, but nobody listened.

"Help, Professor Coateloch!" she called out, but she couldn't see the professor or the inspector anywhere.

The next thing she knew, she was being shoved out of the train station, through the rain, toward a black car that was idling at the curbside with dark smoke drifting from its exhaust pipe.

The spotty girl opened the back door, which strangely opened backward instead of forward. She put Maddy's backpack on the seat and waited. But just as the big girl, with Maddy on her shoulder, reached the car, she tripped, and they both went sprawling across the pavement.

Maddy landed on her bottom but was up on her feet in an instant. She scrambled away from clutching hands and ran back toward the railway station as fast as she could, yelling and screaming at the top of her lungs.

People were starting to stare.

"Help! I'm being kidnapped!" she shouted.

Everybody was looking at her now. A man who was wearing a baseball cap stepped toward her.

"Help!" she yelled, but even as she said it, a strong hand clamped over her mouth and an arm picked her up off the ground. It was the big girl. She was very strong, and Maddy could do nothing as she was carried back to the car.

She saw the man in the cap begin to run after them. He was almost there in time. Almost. He reached the car just as it took off, the tires spinning on the road. Maddy heard and felt the man's hands bang on the side of the car, but they were already speeding away down the street.

"Help!" Maddy cried out, but she knew it was no use.

Still, she had to try.

"Help! Help me!"

CHAPTER FOURTEEN

THE HOUSE

"LET ME GO!" Maddy shouted, but her words were muffled by the dusty old carpet on the floor of the car. Her shock and fear were giving way to anger. "Let me up!"

It was a strange old car. The seats were up on metal legs, like chairs, and the front seat was a single long bench, not two individual seats like in modern cars. She could see right under the seat to where the pimply girl's feet were pressing on pedals as the car drove off through the town. There were three pedals, not two like in Maddy's dad's car. She thought about crawling under the seat and grabbing the girl's feet, but that might have caused an accident and in any case, the big girl wasn't letting her go anywhere.

"Don't let her go until we get out of the city. We don't want anybody to see her," Spotty said.

She was speaking a strange language that Maddy had

never heard before. It was full of odd hissing sounds that made her spine crawl.

"Let me go!" Maddy screamed.

"Be quiet!" the big girl said — in English this time.

"I won't!" Maddy screamed, thrashing about on the floor of the car. The girl was strong, but it was all she could do to keep Maddy down.

"Keep her mouth shut," Spotty said in the strange language. "I'm trying to concentrate on the road."

"I'm trying," the big girl said.

"If you hadn't let her go, then we wouldn't have this problem now, would we, Pavla?" Spotty said.

"I was tripped," Pavla said.

"You're such a klutz," the spotty girl said. "Wait till I tell Mother she almost got away."

There was an awkward silence. "I'm sorry, Anka," Pavla said. "Please don't say anything to Mother."

"I'll think about it," Anka said.

They drove into the mountains. Maddy knew that because they kept going uphill, and quite steeply in some places. After a while, Pavla let her sit up.

There were no other cars around, nor were there any houses. There was nobody to see her. She could scream all she wanted, but there was nobody around to hear her.

"Check her backpack," Anka said.

Pavla picked up Maddy's backpack. "Why?" she asked.

"Leave that alone. It's mine!" Maddy cried.

"Maybe she's hiding something," Anka said.

"Leave it alone," Maddy said again, grabbing the bag and pulling it. Pavla pulled back and pushed Maddy away while she unzipped the top of the backpack.

"Yuck, it stinks in here," Pavla said.

Maddy was sure Mr. Chester was about to be discovered, but there was nothing. No cries of surprise or astonishment. No screeches from the little monkey.

"Just clothes," Pavla said, poking around in the backpack but clearly not wanting to probe too deeply.

Mr. Chester must have burrowed to the very bottom.

Pavla screwed up her nose and pushed the bag back over to Maddy, who quickly zipped it shut.

The road was deserted. A narrow, gravel lane. The trees grew so tall on either side of the road that they blocked out the light. They drove in cold shadows. This part of Bulgaria was not bright and cheerful like the other places she had seen. It was stark, dark, and frightening.

They emerged onto an even narrower road that skirted around the mountainside, dropping away on the other side into a deep ravine. Anka took the corners carefully, and Maddy could see why. The cliff was steep, and the guardrails on the side of the road looked flimsy. It would be a long way to fall.

A set of keys hung from the dashboard on a key chain in the shape of a skull. It was made from shiny metal and jangled against the dashboard.

Eventually, they arrived at imposing black metal gates, which Anka opened by pressing a button on a remote control attached to the key chain.

To Maddy, some houses seemed to be happy, with fresh paint and bright windows like smiling eyes and lace curtains puffing out gently in the breeze. Other houses seemed dour and sullen, watching you go by with a sour expression. This house looked mean. It looked angry, Maddy thought, as they bounced up a long, winding, and bumpy driveway through shady and overgrown gardens that had gone to ruin. They passed a graveyard with crumbling headstones, some of them cracked and others broken, lying in pieces on the ground.

The house was old, made of stone and black-painted wood, with a narrow porch that looked like the muzzle of a dog. Wooden spikes hung from the front of the roof over the porch. They looked like fangs. The house had two turrets like the ones you see in a castle: tall, round stone towers with narrow slits for windows. Black, creeping vines twisted up around the turrets and windows of the house. In front of the house, the driveway made a circle around a dead tree that reached desperate, spindly branches up to the sky.

Just looking at the house, Maddy was scared. But as the two girls hustled her out of the car and hauled her in through the gaping jaws of the house, a strange thing happened. The house shivered. It was no more than a sudden rattling sound from the sides of the house as if the wind had caught some shutters, but still, Maddy couldn't help feeling that as afraid as she was of this creepy old house, it was afraid of her, too.

Maddy pulled her backpack to her as she was marched into the house, feeling the tiny movements of Mr. Chester inside, which gave her a small feeling of hope. A sense that she was not totally alone.

Inside, the house smelled of must and decay. Anka and Pavla pushed and prodded Maddy along a narrow hallway lined with dark wood. Thick cobwebs hung from every corner. A grandfather clock sat at the end of the hallway. As she was marched down the passage, the hands on the clock ticked over to ten o'clock and it began to chime the hours, filling the hallway with noise.

Maddy was taken into a kitchen that looked as though it hadn't been used in years. Spiderwebs covered pots, pans, and long kitchen utensils that were hanging from racks. Something green and gray was growing out of a pot on the stovetop and crawling across the kitchen counter. The clock continued its ominous chime. The sound reverberated around the kitchen, and Maddy was glad when it sounded for the tenth time and finally stopped.

Pavla held Maddy tightly while Anka picked up the handset of an old black phone on a small table by the kitchen door. She dialed a number, and when someone answered, she said simply, "She's here." She hung up the phone without saying goodbye.

A narrow door at the back of the kitchen led to a cellar, down rotten wooden steps that creaked and cracked even under Maddy's light weight. Anka shoved her at the top of the stairs and Maddy stumbled down a few steps, getting a face full of old cobwebs as she did so, before catching her balance with one arm on the old stone wall.

"What are you doing?" she cried out.

"Wait," said Anka.

"Wait for what?" Maddy asked.

"For Mother," Anka said.

"For Mother," Pavla repeated.

The door slammed shut. The only light in the cellar came from a tiny bulb at the end of a cable hanging from the ceiling. It was old and cast only a dim light, just enough to push the darkness back into the corners of the cellar.

She opened her backpack, and Mr. Chester scampered out, climbing up her arm onto her shoulder and rubbing her head with his tiny hands.

"I'm glad you're here," Maddy whispered.

She sat on the second step from the bottom and looked around the confines of the cellar. It was only the size of a small bedroom and was empty except for the rotten remains of two barrels over against the far wall. Outside she heard the black car start up and drive off.

Mr. Chester clung tightly to her neck, and they sat together in the dim light of the cellar.

People would be looking for her. She was sure of that. Professor Coateloch would be frantic. The police would be involved — people had seen her being kidnapped. Perhaps the man in the baseball cap had seen the license plate.

She had no watch, but every hour the old grandfather clock at the end of the hallway chimed. It was after midday when she heard the car returning. That sound was followed by the banging of a door and the clomping of heavy shoes on the floorboards above her head.

That had to be Mother. Surely.

She didn't know whether to be relieved or afraid. At least she could now get out of this dank cellar, but she was terrified of what Mother wanted to do with her. Maddy started to shiver, and before she knew it, tears were welling up in her eyes and she was crying. She kept crying until it hurt her to breathe. Salty tears found their way into her nose and her mouth, and snot dripped down over her lips until she wiped it away with the back of her arm.

She felt a small hand on the back of hers, and Mr. Chester began to chirp softly. Maddy smiled through the tears and Mr. Chester hopped down to the next step.

He chirped again and again, creating a little rhythm with the sounds. Then, like he had at the airport, he began to dance. This time he danced alone, but Maddy's crying stopped as she watched him. After a minute, she started to sing a popular song that was often played on the radio. She sang, and he danced, and Maddy felt that somehow everything was going to turn out all right. Then Mr. Chester climbed up on her shoulder and put his arms back around her neck.

They sat in the cellar.

They waited.

For Mother.

CHAPTER FIFTEEN

THE WITCH

MADDY SAT AT A TABLE in the kitchen. Grime on the windows turned the light from outside into a motley patchwork of gray shades. There was a nasty smell in the air, as if something had gone bad long ago, and the smell still lingered.

Outside, the wind moaned and sighed. And every now and then, in some far-off place, the house would rattle as it had when Maddy arrived.

Maddy sat alone at one end of the table and stared at the witch. She didn't want to stare, but it was hard to take her eyes off the strange tall woman who leaned back in her chair with her hands loosely clasped on her lap.

There was no doubt that she was a witch. Or at least that she looked like one. The real kind of witch, like in the old stories — not the funny ones with big noses and cone-shaped hats that rode broomsticks in movies and fairy tales.

The witch had skin so light that it seemed to shine from under the hood of her cape. Her lips were the color of dried blood and stood out against her pale skin like a piece of coal in a snowy field. They were pursed in a pleasant but rather narrow smile.

Her eyes were small and different colors: one was almost black, the other a vivid green. From her head to her toes, a brown cape fell on top of a brown dress made from a heavy velvet material that flowed like molasses down her body. She wore dark brown nail polish, and she smelled of chocolate: the dark, bitter kind that you use in baking.

She reached up and pulled back the hood of her cape, and Maddy was surprised to see that she had almost no hair. She was completely bald except for one clump on the top of her head at the back that grew long, thick, and black, like the tail of a pony.

"Hello, Maddy," said the witch.

Maddy didn't reply. She didn't want to show the witch how scared she was, and she was sure that if she said anything, her voice would be just a quiet little thing trembling in the still air of the kitchen.

The witch's daughters circled around behind Maddy,

making her uncomfortable. They had removed their black wigs and goth makeup and changed their clothes. Out of their disguises, they no longer looked like sisters. In most ways, they seemed opposites. Pavla was wearing cutoff jeans and a T-shirt and looked like any other ordinary teenager, while Anka wore a dark dress with strange designs on it. Pavla was quite pretty with light, almost blond hair. Anka's hair was black, short, and spiky with a dyed red patch at the front.

Pavla wore earrings that glinted like diamonds, even in the meager light from the window, and she wore a light perfume. Anka had a nose piercing — a silver ring — and another through her right eyebrow. She smelled as though she didn't shower very often.

But the biggest difference between them was their attitudes. Pavla looked uncomfortable. Anka strutted around the room as if she owned it.

"My dear Maddy, you look terrified," the witch said. "But there's no reason to be. You're safe now."

What does she mean "now"? Maddy wondered. She felt very far from safe and wished she were back home in England — or anywhere else in the world, in fact, other than in this strange and creepy old house talking to a witch.

But she was confused as well as afraid, so she found her voice. When it emerged, it was confident and clear, but she still didn't really feel that way. "You had no right to kidnap me," she said. She folded her arms across her chest. "I demand to go home immediately."

"Of course, of course," said the witch, unclasping her hands and leaning forward. "We'll have you safely back home with your mother and father as quickly as we can. But first we had to get you away from that evil professor, and we have to get you home without her finding you."

"Professor Coateloch?" Maddy gasped. "Evil?"

The witch looked at her two daughters. Anka nodded in agreement, as if it was sad but true. Pavla did nothing.

"You have no idea of the danger you were in," the witch said.

"The professor was just pretending to be your friend," Anka said.

"Just pretending," Pavla said.

"You were lucky that you never made it out to the island," the witch said. "If you had, well . . . let's just say it would not have been a fairy-tale ending."

"I really don't know what you're talking about," Maddy said. "At least she didn't kidnap me."

"We didn't kidnap you," Anka said. "We rescued you."

"Yes, we rescued you," Pavla said.

"I don't think you would have come with us any other way," the witch said.

"I might have if . . ." Maddy started, but then stopped. It was probably true. If strangers had approached her at the train station with such an outrageous story, she wouldn't have taken their word for it.

"If what?" the witch asked.

Maddy shook her head. "Who are you?" she asked.

The witch smiled. "My name is rather long and rather old, so I don't use it very often. My friends call me the Chocolate Witch."

Maddy said nothing.

"I hope you'll be my friend, Maddy," the witch said. "I know it will take some time before you trust me, but I'm sure that we'll eventually be friends."

Maddy wasn't so sure about that, or whether she had been rescued or in fact kidnapped. But it seemed best to be polite — for now at least.

"Why the Chocolate Witch?" Maddy asked.

"Because I'm such a sweetie." The witch laughed.

The girls both smiled and nodded.

The witch winked at Maddy and added, "And I do love to eat chocolate."

"Me too," Maddy said, still unsure. The witch seemed nice enough. "Are you honestly a witch?"

"Of course she's a witch," Anka said, as if it was a stupid question.

The witch stood and stepped away from the table. She clapped her hands together three times, and on the third time, when she opened them, her fingertips began to glitter. A stream of butterflies poured out of the gap between her palms. Colorful, brilliant butterflies, all different shapes and sizes. They circled around the room, brightening it, and making a dizzying kaleidoscope of colors and patterns.

"Wow!" said Maddy.

The witch clapped her hands twice more, and the butterflies all turned into white doves, twisting and turning over each other, jostling for space as they flocked around the inside of the room.

Maddy watched, awestruck. She squealed and ducked her head as one of the doves flew right at her. It didn't touch her but just passed through her as if it was made of air. Another clap and the doves disappeared.

"That really was magic!" Maddy said.

"That was nothing. Just a little bit of conjuring." The witch smiled.

"I don't mean to be rude," Maddy said, warming to the rather odd woman. "But why do you live in this funny old house? And . . ." She hesitated. "What happened to your hair?"

"This is my family home," the witch said. "Although, sadly it is falling into disrepair. The cost of maintaining a house like this is enormous, and to be honest, we are not rich. As for my hair, it is the unfortunate result of a simple spell gone wrong. I was trying to get rid of a few pesky gray hairs. I'm afraid I got rid of a few too many."

"I think it's quite distinctive," said Anka.

"Yes, it suits you," Pavla said, which earned her a sharp glance from her mother.

"What about Professor Coateloch? Is she a witch too?" Maddy asked.

"No, Maddy," the witch said. "But I think she wants to be one. I think that's why she wanted you to translate *The Paths of Ancient Magic*."

"But you said she was evil. So she wouldn't be a good witch, would she?"

"I'm afraid not, Maddy," the witch said. "She's not even really a professor, you know."

"She's not?"

The witch shook her head. "No, she —"

She was interrupted by the arrival of a scrawny black cat that had slunk into the kitchen behind them. It jumped up onto the table in front of the witch and regarded Maddy for a moment. Its fur was patchy and matted. Like the witch, it had mismatched eyes — one black and one a vivid green. That was a strange coincidence. The cat sniffed in Maddy's direction, and then curled up on the witch's lap. The witch stroked it gently, and the cat began to purr, but the sound was not like that of other cats. This purr sounded like fingernails scraping over a cheese grater.

"How do you know all this about the professor?" Maddy asked.

"It doesn't matter how I know," the witch said. "What matters is that you are safe now."

But was she safe? Maddy wasn't sure what — or who — to believe. She looked at the witch's daughters who both smiled at her.

"I want to go home now," Maddy said.

"Of course," the witch said. "You can leave anytime you want, but whatever happens, you cannot let the professor find you. I have a friend in the police force who can take you safely back to Sofia. She will be here soon. But you must not show your face to anyone else. There has not been a tongue talker in the world for hundreds, maybe thousands of years, and there are others, not just the professor, who would use your talents for evil."

"A tongue talker?" Maddy asked.

"That is what you are," the witch said. "A talker of tongues. A person who can speak or read any language." The witch stopped talking and regarded Maddy carefully. "It is true, isn't it, Maddy? You are a tongue talker, aren't you?"

"I think so," Maddy said.

"Then it is a rare talent you have," the witch said.

"Thank you," Maddy said.

"Tell her about the old papers," Anka said.

"Yeah, tell her about the old papers," Pavla said.

The witch shook her head.

"What old papers?" Maddy asked.

"Just some old junk we found in the attic," the witch said. "Some very old papers that used to belong to my mother and, I think, her mother before that. In fact, we're not sure how old they are."

"Old papers?" Maddy said, fascinated.

"They are written in an ancient language that we can't understand," the witch said. "I was just going to throw them out."

"I'll go get them," Anka said.

"No, no, I don't want to bother Maddy with this," the witch said.

"Oh please, Mother," Pavla said, and there was something a little odd about the way she said it, but Maddy couldn't put her finger on why.

"My police officer friend will be here any minute," the witch said. "I don't think we have time."

"That's okay," Maddy said. "I'll have a quick look at them before she arrives."

Anka disappeared and returned a moment later with an old leather-bound case that she laid carefully on the table in front of the witch. The witch picked up the cat and put it on the floor. It glared at Maddy, as if somehow it was her fault that it had lost its position on the witch's lap. It slunk off into a corner and began cleaning itself.

The witch pulled the case closer, unlocked it, then reached inside and pulled out a rolled up piece of paper. It did look extremely old and not like any paper that Maddy had ever seen before.

The witch unrolled it and placed it on the table, weighing down the corners with small black stones that she produced from a pocket in her dress.

"Come and sit here," the witch said, and Maddy moved to sit beside her.

"This is one of the papers," the witch said. "It could be anything. It might be a prayer sheet, or a recipe, or even a letter."

It was old, Maddy saw. Much older than the witch had indicated. Maybe much older than the witch knew.

The letters were similar to the strange squiggles that the professor had shown her. Glagolitic she had called the alphabet.

"It's none of those things," Maddy said, twisting and turning her head to bring the letters into focus.

"Well, what is it?" the witch asked.

"It's a magic spell," Maddy said.

For some reason, the witch and her daughters didn't seem surprised.

CHAPTER SIXTEEN

THE SPELLS

IT WAS A SPELL, but it was also some kind of recipe, Maddy realized as she read the words on the crumbly paper.

"It's a recipe for a thunderstorm," Maddy said. "A spell to conjure up a storm."

"I wondered if they were spells," the witch said. "My mother was also a witch, and her mother before her. The 'Recipe for a Thunderstorm' is a simple child's spell that all witches learn when they are young."

"Really," Maddy said.

"I'd love to hear some of it," said the witch. "To see if it is the same as the one I was taught."

"I'm not sure I should," Maddy said.

"Just a little bit," the witch said. "I can even tell you how it starts. 'With a pail of ice and a pitcher of warm water . . .' Am I right?"

Maddy read the first few lines. She nodded.

The witch was smiling at her pleasantly, but Anka was glaring at her. Pavla was looking at the floor, the ceiling — anywhere but at Maddy.

"Just a few words," the witch said. "The police will be here soon."

Maddy read the next few lines out loud.

"It's wonderful to hear those old words," the witch said. "It is the same spell we know today, but somehow the wording seems a little more . . . quaint." She handed Maddy another roll of paper. "What about this one?"

"The calling of the animals," Maddy read aloud without thinking about what she was doing. "If you call a wild animal by its true name, it will come to your bidding. These are the true names of the animals." She read out a few of them and then stopped. "I'm not really sure I should be doing this."

"And this one," the witch asked, handing her another scroll.

"I'm sorry," Maddy said, "but I don't think I should translate any more spells for you. I hardly know you."

"Oh, that's ridiculous," the witch said.

"Absurd," Anka said.

"The taking of tongues," Maddy said eventually, then

stopped. The other spells had sounded interesting and not too dangerous. But this did not sound nice. Far from it. "What does it mean, the taking of tongues?"

"That's a very long story," the witch said.

"I'm sorry, but I'm not going to translate any more spells for you until you tell me," said Maddy, pushing herself back from the table.

The witch's eyes flashed fire, but she took a deep breath and shut them. When she opened them again, they were calm. It reminded Maddy of someone, but she couldn't think whom.

"That is not your concern," the witch said. "I can assure you it is nothing bad."

She was lying. Maddy didn't know how she knew it, but she did. There was a restless excitement in the way the witch was looking at Maddy, then down at the paper, then back to Maddy.

Anka, too, had drawn closer, captivated somehow by the pieces of paper that lay in front of her. Pavla hovered near the door.

"I'm sorry," Maddy said. "But I won't do any more. I want to talk to my parents and the police first. Then I can come back here another day, if you like, and —"

"Of course, of course," the witch said. She was

practically salivating, staring at the scrolls. "As soon as we can. But first read me this spell."

She was no longer asking, Maddy noted. She was demanding. That made Maddy's temper start to rise.

"No, I won't," Maddy said. "I didn't ask to come here, and I want to go home. I'll take the scrolls with me if you want and —" Her mouth dropped open, suddenly horrified.

"Just read the first line," the witch said.

"These are parchment scrolls! They aren't yours at all, are they?" Maddy shouted. "You didn't find them in your attic — they are the scrolls from the monastery! You stole them, and you kidnapped me to translate them for you."

The witch said nothing. Neither did her daughters.

"I won't," Maddy said. She stamped her foot on the floor. "I won't do it. You have to let me go now. I won't translate any more spells for you."

"I think you will," the witch said, her voice a foreboding, low rasp, not at all like the voice she had been using up until now. Her one green eye seemed to glow, and her long fingernails seemed to stretch out into claws, although that was probably just Maddy's imagination.

"I won't — not even if you turn me into a toad,"

Maddy said, wondering why the witch was so desperate to translate the scrolls. What did they contain?

"A toad?" Anka said. "A toad? I think that is a very good idea, don't you, Mother?"

"I won't be able to translate any spells for you if I am a toad, will I?" Maddy said.

"Oh, it won't be *you* we will turn into a toad," Anka said. She nodded at Pavla, and they both disappeared into the room next door.

"I hoped we might be able to do this the nice way," the witch said, "but you are leaving me with little choice."

The girls returned with another person, writhing and struggling in their hands, his mouth covered by a coarse cloth gag.

"Kazuki!" Maddy cried. "What? How?"

"Now read that spell or the next time you see your little Japanese friend, it will be on a lily pad, catching flies with his tongue," Anka snarled.

Kazuki's eyes stared out from above the rough material. He looked terrified even though he had no idea what the girl was saying.

"I'll count to three," the witch said.

Maddy stared at Kazuki in shock. All the anger fizzled

out of her. She couldn't let any harm come to him. Slowly, sadly, Maddy's eyes dropped toward the dusty old scroll weighed down at the four corners by the witch's black stones.

For the first time in her life, the ability to speak another language felt like a burden on her shoulders — a curse instead of a blessing.

"You're going to go to jail for this," Maddy said.

"Just translate the spell," Anka hissed.

"As soon as I get out of here, I'm going to the police, and they're going to lock you up for a really long time," Maddy said.

The witch stabbed a bony finger at the scroll in front of her. "Now," she said.

Maddy paused, and then she began unwillingly, "You need a morsel of dragon's tongue . . ."

CHAPTER SEVENTEEN

KAZUKI

THE DOOR TO THE CELLAR shut above them with a thud. The single hanging light bulb shuddered and dim shadows danced across the stone walls.

For over an hour the witch had forced Maddy to read the spells aloud while she and her daughters copied down the incantations and ingredients. Some were odd recipes, like the recipes for thunderstorms and quicksand. Others were to control plants, or the stars, or the tides. Some made no sense to Maddy at all, but all of them, she was now convinced, were evil. This was the black magic she had been warned about.

Maddy helped Kazuki pull off his gag, then she wrapped her arms around him and gave him a huge hug. He hugged her back tightly.

He started to say something, but Maddy pressed her

finger to her lips to stop him, waiting until she heard the footsteps at the top of the stairs recede.

"What are you doing here?" Maddy asked. She wasn't sure if she should be angry with him, surprised, or relieved that he was okay. "Why did you sneak away from the police at the airport?"

"I promised you I wasn't going to let anything bad happen to you," Kazuki said. "How could I keep that promise if I had gone back to England?"

Maddy had been going to say something else but stopped. There was a word, she thought, to describe what Kazuki had done, but even with all the languages she could speak, she couldn't find the right one. The closest she could come up with was "noble."

"But how did you get here?" she asked.

"We had to wait at the airport for a lady from the Japanese Embassy to arrive," Kazuki said. "And when she came, they were all busy trying to sort out the flights or something, and while they were doing that, I went invisible and just snuck away."

Maddy knew that Kazuki didn't really go invisible, he was just good at not being seen, but she didn't say anything.

"I knew you were going to Burgas," Kazuki continued,

"so I found a train that was going there and got on it while they were all still looking for me."

"But you didn't have a train ticket."

Kazuki shook his head. "Nobody asked me for one. But when I got to Burgas I didn't know what to do next. I couldn't find out how to get to Sozopol, and I didn't want to go back to Sofia, so I stayed at the train station. I slept on the floor in a quiet corner where nobody could see me."

"That doesn't sound very comfortable," Maddy said.

"It wasn't," Kazuki agreed. "It was cold and hard, and I was hungry and thirsty. I knew they must be looking for me. The next morning I saw a police officer, and I was about to go and tell him who I was when I saw that you and the professor were with him. Then I saw those two nasty girls kidnap you."

"You saw that?" Maddy said. "Why didn't you do anything?"

"I did!" Kazuki said. "I tripped up the big girl just as she got to the car."

"That was you?" said Maddy.

"Yes, but then they caught you again, and I didn't know what else to do, so I hid in the car."

"You were in the car with us?" Maddy was more and more astounded by Kazuki's talent for not being seen.

"Yes. While they were chasing you, I climbed into the car and hid under the backseat," Kazuki said.

"But I was on the floor, too," she said.

Kazuki smiled. "If you had turned around, you would have seen me," he said. "I was right behind you."

"So what happened next?" Maddy asked.

"I waited in the car until I thought it was quiet outside. But when I opened the door, the spotty-faced girl was right there. I think she got just as big of a scare as I did when the door opened. But she yelled out for the other girl, and they grabbed me. They tied me up and gagged me and locked me in a back bedroom."

"They thought they'd use you to get me to do what they wanted," Maddy said, shaking her head. "And it worked."

"I'm sorry, Maddy." Kazuki looked like he was going to cry.

Maddy had to take a deep breath so that she didn't cry too. "You shouldn't be sorry," Maddy said. "You are a hero. A real ninja hero."

Kazuki's face brightened when she said that. "Am I?" he asked doubtfully.

"Yes," Maddy said. "And a very good friend." That reminded her of Mr. Chester.

"Mr. Chester," she whispered, but there was no sudden scampering of tiny feet, no tug on her clothes as he climbed up onto her shoulder. "Mr. Chester?" she said again, but still there was nothing. She checked her backpack, but it was empty.

"Who is Mr. Chester?" Kazuki asked.

Kazuki hadn't seen Mr. Chester at the airport, Maddy realized, and he certainly wouldn't know that the sneaky little fellow had stowed away in her backpack. She quickly explained all that and how she thought Mr. Chester had somehow been sent by Dimitar's father to look after her and that he was probably part magic, but Kazuki looked very doubtful about that.

Where was the little monkey? He wasn't anywhere in the cellar, and the door at the top of the stairs had been shut the whole time, so he couldn't have gotten out.

Then again, Maddy thought, a monkey who could free himself from an animal cage in the cargo hold of an airplane and get into her backpack was capable of anything.

They waited in the gloom of the cellar on the bottom step, which was the only place to sit. Kazuki took Maddy's hand and held it, but she wasn't sure if he was holding it to reassure her or himself.

"Listen," Maddy said.

A light tapping sound, barely audible, was coming from somewhere in the cellar.

"Did you hear that?" Maddy asked.

Kazuki nodded.

The tapping continued.

"What is it?" Maddy asked.

"I don't know," Kazuki said. He looked small and frightened. They were both glad when it stopped.

There were discussions going on upstairs, but in quiet voices, so although they could hear people talking, they couldn't make out the words. Then they heard the witch's car start up. It hiccupped a couple of times, then it drove off down the gravel driveway.

"They left!" Kazuki said. "We have to get out of here before she casts some kind of spell on us."

"But we don't know who's still here," Maddy said.

"We have to try to escape," Kazuki said.

"How?" Maddy asked.

Kazuki looked around. The walls of the cellar were thick blocks of stone. The only entrance was by the door at the top of the stairs. There was no way out.

After a while, they heard the click of a key in the lock and the cellar door opened. The light from the kitchen fell

down into the murky gloom of the cellar — just a narrow strip but enough to push away the shadows.

A shape blocked the light. It was the big girl — Pavla. She stood in the doorway, making sure there was no possibility of escape.

Maddy stood and turned to face her. Kazuki moved half a step in front of her. He raised his fists into a karate stance. "Leave her alone, you big bully," he said. "I'm not afraid of you."

Maddy was watching Pavla's face, and what she saw was not threatening or cruel. She touched Kazuki lightly on the arm.

"It's all right, Kazuki," she said. "She's not going to hurt us."

"How do you know?" Kazuki said while making punching and blocking moves with his arms. The sleeves of his black ninja suit swished with the rapid movements.

"Because she's different from the others," Maddy said.

Pavla shook her head and sat down on the top step, still blocking the doorway in case they tried to escape. She said nothing.

Maddy stared at her. At first she had thought Pavla wasn't very bright because of the slow way that she spoke and the way that she seemed to repeat things her sister had said. But now she didn't think that was right. It was more that Pavla knew what she wanted to say — it just took her longer than most people to work out how to say it.

She was nothing like her sister. It was hard to believe they were even related. Anka seemed a lot like their mother. Maybe Pavla took after their father.

"Where are the others?" Maddy asked.

"Mother has gone out," Pavla said. A long pause. "Anka, too."

"Where have they gone?" Maddy asked.

"To get dragon's tongue," Pavla said. Another pause. "It's very rare nowadays."

Maddy translated the conversation for Kazuki, who said, "Dragon's tongue? Is that real?"

"I don't know," Maddy said.

Pavla obviously wanted to tell them something but was struggling to find the right words.

"You're not like your sister," Maddy said.

Pavla shook her head with a quiet smile.

"Maybe you take after your father," Maddy said.

Pavla shook her head sadly. "Maybe," she said after a little deliberation.

Then, for the first time, Maddy saw the sun shine out of Pavla's face. "Father was tall and very handsome," she said. "He was kind, and he told wonderful, funny stories."

"My dad does, too," Maddy said. "Where was your father from?"

"I think Mother . . . I think she magicked him," said Pavla.

"You mean she created him out of thin air?" Kazuki asked after Maddy had translated. He finally dropped his arms from their defensive position and took a step backward.

Pavla shook her head. "No. He was from a nearby town. I think Mother made a love spell to make him fall in love with her."

"Could she really do that?" Maddy asked.

"Love spells are easy," she said. "Like conjuring butterflies. Anyone can do it. And the person under the spell thinks they are actually . . ." her voice tightened, "in love with you."

"So what happened?" Kazuki asked. "Did she turn him into a . . . something?"

That made Pavla smile again, but you could feel the heartbreak behind it. "When he disappeared," Pavla said, "that's what I thought, too. I was only little, and I thought she had turned him into something else. Every time I saw a bird or a dog or a nice flower, I would look at it closely to see if it was him. But that's big magic. She can't do big magic."

Pavla shifted around uncomfortably on the hard wooden step. "When I got a little older, I realized that he had just gone away. He must have been so frightened of her that he ran away." She dropped her eyes. "He never said goodbye . . ." Her voice trailed off.

"Please let us go," Maddy said. "We've done nothing wrong."

Pavla shook her head again. "I can't." She faltered around for a bit, trying to put words together, and finally looked at Kazuki. "Why did you come here?" she asked. "That's what I came down to ask. Why did you hide in the car and come up here?"

Maddy translated the question for Kazuki.

"Because she's my friend," Kazuki said.

Pavla was silent for a moment. She said, "You are lucky, Maddy, to have a friend like Kazuki."

"I know," Maddy said, putting her arm around Kazuki's shoulders.

"And he is lucky to have a friend like you," Pavla said.

"Please let us go," Maddy asked again.

"I can't," Pavla said.

"Let us go!" Kazuki shouted, but as he said it there was the sound of a car, and Pavla jumped straight up into the air as if a wasp had stung her.

She raced back up the stairs, and the door slammed shut. A thin veil of dust wafted down in the meager light from the cellar bulb.

"Maddy —" Kazuki began, but he was interrupted by the sound of knocking. Someone was at the front door!

Both of them strained their ears toward the ceiling.

The knock sounded again, and they could hear footsteps above them as Pavla went to answer it.

The creak of the door was audible from the cellar.

"Hello?" said Pavla.

Maddy recognized the next voice instantly. It was a deep, gravelly voice that reverberated through the floorboards above them.

"Excuse me, young lady. I'm sorry for the intrusion, but I'm looking for my father's monkey."

CHAPTER EIGHTEEN

DIMITAR THE GIANT

"DIMITAR! DIMITAR!" Maddy screamed. She screwed up her face and let out a high-pitched squeal. "Dimitar!" she yelled again, and this time Kazuki joined in with her.

They could hear shouting, then heavy footsteps above their heads. Suddenly, the cellar door thrust open, banging back against the wall, and Dimitar the Giant stood in the doorway. He shook his head, perplexed.

"Little Maddy!" he said. "What are you doing here?"

Pavla appeared behind Dimitar. She leaped up onto his back and wrapped her arms around his head, wrestling with him. She was big and strong, but he hardly seemed to notice. He just shook his shoulders and dismissed her as easily as brushing off a fly.

"We've been kidnapped!" Maddy said. "By a witch."

"A witch?"

"Yes!"

Dimitar didn't laugh or doubt her. "Where is she?"

"She drove off to get something," Maddy said.

"In a black car?" Dimitar asked.

"Yes!"

"I just passed a car like that. We must hurry before she gets back," Dimitar said.

"No," Pavla screamed. "You can't go. If Mother returns and you're gone . . ."

"You should run away too," Maddy said.

Dimitar turned and led the way to the door.

"No!" Pavla hurled herself at him again, but he fended her off with a huge hand, and she fell back onto one of the kitchen chairs with a thud, looking distraught.

"Come on," Dimitar growled, and Maddy and Kazuki scrambled up the stairs.

"How did you know we were here?" Maddy asked.

"I didn't," Dimitar said, shoving the kitchen table out of the way as he took the shortest path to the hallway door. "I was looking for Mr. Chester."

"Mr. Chester! How did you know he was here?" Maddy asked.

"He called me."

"He *called* you?"

"Yes. I could hear him chirping on the end of the line, and I knew right away it was him. A friend of mine at the telephone company traced the number to this address."

Mr. Chester had called Dimitar!

That was unbelievable, Maddy thought, until she remembered that Mr. Chester had been trained to dial the phone for Dimitar's father, who would have called Dimitar lots of times. The clever little monkey must have remembered the number.

"Come on, let's take you home," Dimitar said. But now there was a dark shape in front of them.

"It's the witch!" Maddy screamed.

"Out of my way," the giant stormed, but the witch was muttering in that low rasp.

A spider dropped from the ceiling onto Dimitar's back. It was huge, with long, furry legs and a body as big as Maddy's hand.

"There's a spider on your back," Maddy yelled.

Dimitar reached around and knocked it off, but it just turned and ran back up his leg. Another spider dropped even as he did so, and another, and another. There were small spiders and big spiders, hundreds of them, dropping from the ceiling, crawling out of the walls, up through the floorboards. Some had yellow-and-black stripes across their bodies. Others were red and black with red joints across their legs. Still others were jet-black with a single yellow stripe. They all looked scary.

Dimitar swept his hands across his back, ridding himself of some of them, but they landed on the floor and ran back at him. His back turned yellow and red and black with the creatures. They were in his long hair and his beard.

The witch continued muttering the spell. It was one of the ones Maddy had translated.

Now Maddy could see what the spiders were doing. They were spinning webs, tiny strands of glittering web, around and around. At first, Dimitar broke the webs and kept on walking toward the witch, but as more and more spiders landed on him and started spinning their webs, he began to slow down, his legs trapped by thousands of strands.

Maddy was screaming, and Kazuki was yelling.

Anka appeared from behind the witch and grabbed Maddy.

She started to haul Maddy back toward the cellar. Pavla caught Kazuki, who struggled furiously but could not break her grip.

Dimitar's arms were now caught in the webs. Every

movement he made was slow and sluggish. Any normal person would have been completely immobilized by now, yet still, somehow, with his tremendous strength, Dimitar kept going. He reached out for the witch.

She sneered at him and ducked beneath his slow, pawing grasp.

He began to topple forward and landed on the floor, spiders scattering in all directions.

A moment later, Maddy and Kazuki were back in the cellar. The door slammed shut above them, and this time, the light was off.

Tap, tap, tap, came the sound they had heard earlier.

Tap, tap, tap . . .

CHAPTER NINETEEN

TAP, TAP, TAP

IN THE BLACKNESS OF THE CELLAR, Maddy's imagination began to create pictures of what she could not see. Cockroaches creeping from tiny holes in the walls of the cellar, spiders crawling across the ceiling, a huge rat emerging from under the stairs, its teeth tapping together as it waited to bite.

Her breath came in short, hard bursts, and she put her hand over her mouth so she wouldn't scream. Maddy tried to tell herself that it was only her imagination. She shut her eyes, but that made no difference. It was just as dark either way, and her imagination kept playing the same tricks on her.

When she thought she could bear it no longer, she heard a quiet click, and then a thin, bluish light lit the inside of the cellar.

"A good ninja is prepared for anything," Kazuki said. He had a small flashlight in his hand.

"Kazuki, you're amazing!" Maddy said. She wondered what else he had hidden in the secret pockets in his ninja suit. She was about to ask him when the noise came again.

Tap, tap, tap. Like fingernails on a table. Or talons on wooden floorboards.

The noise seemed to be coming from under the stairs. Suddenly, she thought of Mr. Chester. Perhaps it was him. Perhaps he was trapped under there.

"Come with me," Maddy said, and after a short hesitation, Kazuki followed her.

She went carefully down to the bottom of the stairs, and Kazuki shined the flashlight around underneath. The space beneath the staircase was dusty and full of cobwebs. The dust on the floor was disturbed, as if some creature had recently been here. There were scratches in the dust that looked like they had been made by claws.

The walls of the cellar were made of stone. But there, on the back wall under the stairs, was a wooden panel . . . and it was there where the tapping sound came from.

Maddy wavered, then slowly pushed on the panel.

"Are you sure you want to do that?" Kazuki asked.

"No," Maddy said, but she pushed on the panel again

anyway. It seemed solid. Kazuki shined his light around the outside of it, but as far as they could see, it fit snugly into the stone that surrounded it.

Still, the tapping noise came from the other side.

"Mr. Chester?" Maddy asked, her voice quivering.

Tap, tap, tap.

"Mr. Chester?"

There were no chirps or screeches from the other side of the panel.

"It's not Mr. Chester," Kazuki said, backing away.

"Bring that light back here," Maddy said.

"It's not Mr. Chester," Kazuki said again. Who knew what kind of horrors awaited them behind a secret panel in the cellar of a witch's house?

There was a hole in the stone wall by the wooden panel. Just a gap where a few of the stones had not fit together properly.

"Shine your light in here," Maddy said, her voice now no more than a whisper.

Kazuki tried, but the flashlight was shaking so badly that the light went everywhere except where Maddy wanted it to go.

"Give me the flashlight," Maddy said, and Kazuki passed it.

She shined it into the hole but could see nothing. Holding her breath, she reached into the hole.

"Maddy, no!" Kazuki cried.

Maddy shut all thoughts out of her mind. Thoughts of rats and snakes and spiders and other sharp-toothed and poisonous creatures whose home she could be putting her hand into. She knew that if she let even a shred of those thoughts into her mind, she would never do what she was doing.

Deeper she reached into the black hole. She bumped her knuckle on a spur of rock but kept going. Her hand touched something smooth. Cold. A piece of metal perhaps. She grasped it and pulled it. There was a click, and a narrow gap appeared down one side of the panel.

"It's a little doorway," Maddy cried.

Kazuki moved closer, fascinated despite his fear. She handed him back the flashlight and pushed on the door. It opened easily, and Kazuki aimed his flashlight inside. The panel concealed a circular tunnel, with walls made of brick.

In the middle, a short way back from the opening, Mr. Chester sat on his haunches, his arms crossed over his chest. The expression on his face was clear: *What took you so long?*

"Mr. Chester!" Maddy cried. "It was you!" She crawled into the tunnel. Kazuki followed her, the flashlight now steadier.

Mr. Chester ran up her arm onto her back, sitting on the back of her neck like a jockey on a horse.

"Where do you think it goes?" Kazuki asked.

"I don't know, but anywhere is better than sitting in that cellar waiting for the witch to return," Maddy said.

The panel clicked shut behind them.

The tunnel was small, just big enough for a grown-up to crawl through, Maddy thought, which meant there was plenty of room for her and Kazuki.

Straight ahead, Maddy could see another panel. On this side was a handle. She turned it cautiously and stayed very still for a moment, watching for any movement, listening for any sound. There was nothing. She edged out through the doorway. Kazuki followed, and the door clicked shut behind them.

They had emerged under another set of stairs. Another cellar, but this was nothing like the last. The room was huge. It stretched out in front of them, a cavern under the earth. The only light came from a high, narrow window at the far end, letting in thin strips of daylight and air but not enough to remove the musty smell of the room.

Along all the walls were shelves full of bottles and glass flasks with cork stoppers in them.

In the center of the room, a pattern of stones on the old stone floor made a strange triangular design. In the middle was a metal cauldron about the size of a large cooking pot.

They were in the witch's lair.

One thing looked out of place, though — a small dressing table with a mirror. On it were little pots and tubes of makeup, a hairbrush, and a long black wig on a stand.

They walked out from under the stairs, and Maddy looked up at a large, heavy door, crisscrossed with metal bands.

"Come on," she whispered. "Let's get out of here."

She began to climb up toward the door, hoping that it wouldn't be locked.

Halfway up the stairs, she stopped. Footsteps sounded on the other side of the door. Kazuki's fingertips dug deeply into her arm.

Then came the rattle of a key in the lock.

CHAPTER TWENTY

THE LAIR

SILENTLY, MADDY, KAZUKI, and Mr. Chester hurried back down the staircase and ran underneath it. There was nowhere else to hide and no time to open the door to the tunnel. They crouched in the darkest corner of the space under the stairs and waited.

They heard the big door open, and then shoes sounded on the steps above them. Dust trickled down, tiny dots of gold in the light from the high window. A pair of heavy brown shoes appeared in the gaps between the boards. Then the long brown dress. The smell of bitter chocolate wafted past. The witch walked to the center of the room. She was carrying a dark brown bag, which she placed on the floor by the cauldron. She looked around, then right at the stairs. Maddy shrank back as far as she could, and the witch's eyes moved on without seeing them.

The witch waved her hands in the air, and her fingertips sparkled. The sparkles seemed to reflect off the ceiling, but then Maddy realized that the ceiling was full of candles. There were hundreds of them hanging from huge chandeliers. As they watched, the sparks from the witch's fingertips flew into the air, lighting the candles. Slowly, the room filled with a pale yellow glow.

The witch twirled her ponytail around into a bun, and secured it with a long hairpin. She scratched absent-mindedly at the bald top of her head. She seemed to be waiting for something.

After a moment, there were running footsteps at the top of the stairs. "They're gone!" It was Anka's voice.

"Gone?"

"The cellar is empty!" Pavla said.

"Pavla didn't lock the door properly," Anka said.

"Me? It was you who shut the door."

"It was you, you idiot."

"Stupid toad of a girl," the witch said. "Go and look for them. Search everywhere."

The sisters disappeared, and the witch was quiet, thinking. She took some papers from the brown bag and consulted them. Maddy didn't have to see them to know what they were. It was the translations. The spells!

The witch began to mutter again, more low, dark sounds, and then sparks flew from her fingertips, brighter than before. A few moments later, there was a scraping sound from the high window, and a huge black crow was perched on the windowsill. It was joined by another, then another. The witch murmured some words to the crows, and they flew off together.

Maddy watched, horrified. Now the witch was casting another spell, and a strange rustling, scratching noise sounded above them. It got louder and louder until it was right overhead. Then a shadow blotted out the light.

Maddy and Kazuki held each other as a dark shape flowed down the stairs in front of them. Maddy's mind could not comprehend the black, shapeless mass that slithered above. What vile creature could this be? What evil had the witch summoned from the depths of the underworld?

The scratching, scrabbling noise was much louder now, and as Maddy watched, a cockroach dropped between the gap in the stair treads onto the box in front of her. Then another. Now hundreds of them were dropping down and running toward the center of the floor.

Mr. Chester was gripping her hair so tightly that he was hurting her. He was terrified, too.

That's what the noise was. Cockroaches. A river of them. Thousands of the creatures crawling down the stairs above her head. Maddy hadn't known there were so many cockroaches in all of existence, let alone all in one place.

Floating along on the cockroaches was a silent, motionless shape. It was only when it reached the cauldron that she saw what it was.

Dimitar!

For a moment, she could see his face, and it was full of fury. He struggled a couple of times against his bonds, but the thick mat of spider webbing held firmly.

The cockroach army stopped. A wave of black bugs rippled out from underneath Dimitar's body, and within a few minutes, all of the cockroaches had disappeared into cracks in the walls and the floor. Dimitar lay in the middle of the cold, hard stone floor and glared at the witch with an expression that would have scared his wrestling opponents right out of the ring. But the witch seemed unconcerned.

"I was going to test one of the spells on the children," the witch said. "But you'll do much better." Dimitar writhed and twisted, his face red as he strained to break the bonds that held him.

"When I get my hands on you . . ." he muttered.

The witch just laughed a low-pitched cackle.

Pavla and Anka returned, shaking their heads.

"They're nowhere in the house," Anka said. "We've looked everywhere."

"It doesn't matter," the witch said. "The only place they can run to is the forest, and they won't get far. I have asked the wild beasts to take care of them."

She leafed slowly through the pages of spells, a smirk coming over her face at some of them.

"Eeeny, meeny, miny, moe," she said. "Catch a giant by the toe."

She selected one of the spells and seemed pleased with her choice.

"Pavla, find me some bat droppings," the witch said. "Third shelf on the right."

Pavla scanned the glass jars and bottles on the shelf until she found it: a small ceramic urn with a cork stopper. She handed it to the witch, who carefully measured out a small amount and put it in the cauldron.

"Sulfur," the witch said, pointing toward one of the shelves.

Anka went to find it.

The witch carefully tapped a few grains into the mixture. The smell of rotten eggs began to waft around the room. She added a few more grains, then again, checking the paper like a recipe until she was satisfied with whatever it was she was doing. Then she picked up a small bowl from a shelf on the far side of the room.

She called the girls over. "Put on your runestones," the witch said. "I don't want you two catching this spell."

Pavla and Anka each took a small, round, smooth pebble from the bowl. The pebbles seemed to glow softly under the light of the candles, and Maddy could see strange markings on them. The stones were attached to thin loops of thread.

The witch did not wear one. Maybe she didn't need to, Maddy thought, as she was the person casting the spell.

Once the girls had placed the runestones around their necks, the witch used the ladle to take a sample of the mixture and pour it into a glass flask. She swirled it around in the flask, sniffed at it, then held it up and looked at the color. How she could see properly in this dim yellow light, Maddy had no idea.

The witch opened a large brown bag that had been sitting on the floor by her feet. She took out a thin glass tube with a cork in the end of it. There was something small, black, and rubbery in the bottom of the tube. Setting the tube down on a small stand, she carefully took out the cork.

A strange sense of darkness invaded the room and, in her mind, although not with her ears, Maddy could hear a distant roaring sound.

Next the witch took a small wooden stick and dipped it in the flask. It emerged, dripping with the vile-looking liquid. She approached Dimitar and motioned the girls to back away.

"Your runestones should protect you but just in case, try not to breathe in any of the smoke," she said.

She snapped her fingers, and a flame appeared between them, which she used to set fire to the end of the small stick. As soon as it was flaming, she blew it out. A thin wisp of yellow-colored smoke drifted from the end of it.

She waved the stick under Dimitar's nose and began to chant ancient words — terrible words. Words that Maddy had translated from the parchment scrolls.

It took only a few moments before Maddy recognized the spell. It was the spell of tongue taking! She was going to steal Dimitar's tongue. Not his real tongue, Maddy knew, but his language, his words, his ability to talk. She usually didn't sweat very much, but now she felt a cold sweat break out around the back of her neck and under her arms.

The smoke wafted toward Dimitar. Although she was

quite a long way from the witch, Maddy instinctively covered her nose.

Dimitar shut his mouth tightly and narrowed his nostrils. He was holding his breath, trying not to breathe in the smoke. But the witch waited, and the smoke continued to drift.

After a few minutes, Dimitar could hold his breath no longer. His face turned red and his eyes bulged out, until he gulped in a huge breath of air and with it, the smoke from the glowing stick.

When he breathed out, the smoke came out too, but it had changed. It was no longer a thin, semitransparent wisp of smoke. Now it seemed thick and lumpy, like bad yogurt.

The smoke swirled toward the small glass tube, settling into a low, dense cloud on the bottom, barely covering the black object. Maddy knew now what that object was: a tiny piece of dragon's tongue.

"Did it work?" Anka asked breathlessly.

"Why don't you ask him?" the Chocolate Witch said, putting the cork back on the glass tube and swirling the pale smoke around inside it. It rose up inside the tube but quickly settled back down to a low cloud on the bottom.

"Go on, say something, tough guy," Anka said, walking up and kicking Dimitar in the leg.

"Aaarrgha, ooorgha, grumph," Dimitar said, and his face strained with the effort. He tried again. *"Oooorrrgh. Aarrrgh. Draaak."* He tried a few more times to talk, but he no longer seemed to be able to make words.

The witch said, "You can babble all you like and nobody will understand you. Nor you them!" She clapped her hands together, threw her head back, and cackled.

"Is it permanent?" Anka asked. She picked up the glass tube and twirled it around, watching the lumpy smoke form into a small whirlpool inside.

"The tongue will seek out its owner if it escapes from the glass," the witch said. "As long as it escapes the same day it was taken."

"The same day?" Pavla asked.

"The same day," the witch said. "A tongue cannot survive long without its owner. Once the clock strikes midnight, it will turn to dust."

"Uuuurrrrgha!" Dimitar said.

"He sounds like a baby." Anka laughed and circled the horizontal giant. "Just a little bubby boy. How cute."

Dimitar looked anything but cute.

"Now I must go and talk to the police again. If I don't show up, they will start to get suspicious."

Maddy mouthed to Kazuki, "Talk to the police?"

Why did the witch want to talk to the police? Were they in on it, too?

"While I am gone, I want you to find those children," the witch said. "Search everywhere. They can't have gone far. They may even be hiding somewhere in the house."

As she said that, her gaze flitted around the room, passing once again right over the stairs where Maddy and Kazuki crouched in the gloom. The witch's green eye burned. Maddy felt it cast an evil light right into the depths of the shadows in which they were hiding, but if she saw them, she said and did nothing.

The two girls disappeared upstairs.

The witch moved over to the small dressing table and sat down. She picked up a brush, dabbled it in a small pot, and started to apply it to her face.

Then something extraordinary happened. Her face began to soften, almost as if it was about to melt. Whatever the makeup was, it was no ordinary makeup. Her face became spongy and rubbery, like modeling clay. Her fingers flitted over her face, pulling a little bit this way, pushing a bit that way, reshaping her nose, the curve of her mouth, the set of her eyes. She kept her eyes on the mirror, checking what she was doing.

She put on a long black wig and brushed it.

Then some more makeup . . . normal makeup this time. Blush and lipstick.

The witch stood and walked toward the stairs. Maddy shrank backward.

The transformation was startling. It was no longer the witch who was walking toward her. It was someone else entirely. Someone whom Maddy knew all too well.

The thin, bony nose was gone, as were the mismatched eyes; they were now an even hazel color. The pale skin was radiant and youthful. Her teeth were perfectly even and white, like the keys of a piano.

The witch stepped lightly over Maddy's head.

"I don't believe it!" Maddy hissed to Kazuki in the faintest of whispers as soon as the door at the top of the stairs closed. But she did believe it because she had seen it with her own eyes.

Now she knew why the witch had to talk to the police. She had to keep up appearances. Professor Coateloch would be doing everything she could to help the police with their search.

But some magic makeup, a long black wig, and a change of clothes, and it wasn't the witch who had walked up the stairs above their heads. It was Professor Coateloch.

Professor Coateloch was the witch.

CHAPTER TWENTY-ONE

ESCAPE

WHEN THE WITCH had gone, and with no sounds from the stairs to indicate that she or the two girls were coming back, Maddy and Kazuki ventured out from their hiding place.

They ran over to Dimitar, who was lying like an Egyptian mummy in swathes of spider webbing. His eyes opened wide at the sight of them and Mr. Chester, who was still perched on Maddy's shoulder.

"*Urgle, urgle, unk!*" he said.

Mr. Chester jumped up and down and chirped at the giant.

"Are you okay?" Maddy asked.

Dimitar just stared at her. He strained against the bindings, but the thick, matted fabric cocooned him tightly, and even his great strength could do nothing.

"Did the witch steal his tongue?" Kazuki asked, horrified.

"Not his actual tongue," Maddy explained. "Tongue means language. She stole his language."

Mr. Chester shook his head, as if in disgust.

"That horrible old witch planned this all along," said Maddy. "But when my parents asked for me to be sent home, that messed everything up, so she kidnapped me instead and stole the scrolls from the monastery."

"What do we do now?" Kazuki asked.

"Find something sharp and cut these webs off him," Maddy said. Maddy and Kazuki hunted around the witch's lair, but they could find nothing sharp enough to cut the spiderwebs.

"We have to get out of here before she comes back," Kazuki said.

"Where? We can't go into the forest," Maddy said. "The witch has called the wild animals to look for us."

Kazuki looked even more terrified than before.

Mr. Chester began rubbing Maddy's head.

"Not now," she said a little irritably, shaking her head.

Mr. Chester perched on her shoulder, put both arms around her neck, and touched his lips to her cheek. A little monkey kiss.

"I'm sorry, Mr. Chester," Maddy said. "I'm just frightened, that's all."

He chirped, as if to say, "That's okay."

"So what do we do?" Kazuki asked again.

Maddy looked at the thick mat of spiderwebs and didn't want to touch it, but when she did, to her surprise, it was not sticky at all. She remembered learning at school that spiderwebs are only sticky on one side.

She pulled at the strands with her bare hands, but the web was too thick and matted.

"It's a shame you don't have a ninja sword," she said to Kazuki, thinking of the fierce men with long swords in the posters on his bedroom wall.

She could see him thinking about that, then he turned and walked over to the shelf of jars and pots. He found a jar that was mostly empty and, before Maddy could say or do anything, he dropped it on the floor.

The crash reverberated around the room, an explosion of sound, and Maddy was sure they must have heard it upstairs. She held her breath, but nobody came to look.

Kazuki picked up the largest piece of glass, which included the unbroken top of the jar. The bottom was a jagged edge, like a knife.

"Quickly!" Maddy said.

Kazuki pressed the broken edge against the webs between Dimitar's legs and sawed back and forth. A small hole appeared. He pressed the point of the glass down into the hole and sawed some more. It was very hard work. The webs were sticky underneath and clung to the glass.

After a few minutes, Maddy took over and cut away as best she could, but it was taking too long. With all their hard work, they had only managed to make a cut in the webbing from just below his knees down to his feet.

"This is taking too long!" Maddy said. "The witch will be back soon."

Dimitar rolled over onto his stomach, and Maddy and Kazuki, between them, managed to cut the same section of webs on the back of Dimitar's legs.

Dimitar grunted a couple of times, and they stopped, unsure what he wanted them to do.

With his face pressed onto the hard rock floor, he brought his knees up underneath him, then lifted himself up until he was kneeling. He rested for a moment, then rocked back on his haunches, balancing carefully. Then he straightened his legs, lifting himself upright.

His hands were still trapped by his side, and his knees were stuck together, but he could walk, in a sense . . . like a duck waddling.

"We need to leave now — before the witch comes back," Maddy said, and the giant looked at her without understanding but followed them to the stairs.

Mr. Chester chirped and began to jump up and down.

"What is it, Mr. Chester?" Maddy asked.

Mr. Chester ran across the floor. He scampered up onto one of the shelves and came running back. In his hand he had three of the runestone necklaces.

"Good boy!" Maddy said. "In case she tries to cast a spell on us. What a clever monkey!"

Mr. Chester hopped from one foot to the other.

Maddy put one on and handed one to Kazuki. Dimitar bowed down, and she managed to tie the other around his big, thick neck.

Dimitar waddled across to the bottom of the stairs and stopped, looking at them. He strained against the webbing and slowly lifted one foot up onto the first step. He leaned forward and, balancing precariously, lifted his other foot up onto the step. It creaked and almost cracked under the weight. Another step and again the creak from the wooden step, louder this time. Footsteps sounded on the floor above them, and they all froze in place. Maddy stared up the staircase at the door, certain that the witch's daughters must have heard them. But the door stayed closed.

"Come on," she said.

One more step, then another. It seemed to take an hour, and Maddy was terrified the whole time that the witch would come back or that the girls would think to check on Dimitar.

Finally, they were at the top of the staircase, and Dimitar paused, trying to get some strength back.

"Wait!" Kazuki said. He ran back down the stairs and grabbed the glass tube full of smoke. It disappeared somewhere into his ninja suit and ran back up the stairs.

They crept down a corridor. Ahead of them, Maddy could hear Pavla.

"We have to hurry," Maddy whispered. She couldn't see or hear Anka anywhere and worried that the witch's daughter might suddenly bump into them.

The narrow corridor joined onto a much wider hallway. Through the door to the kitchen, Maddy could see Pavla. She was on the telephone. She had her back turned to them.

Just as they were passing the kitchen, something moved in front of them. A sinister, scraggly shape uncurled itself from a corner. The witch's cat!

It arched its back and opened its mouth, hissing at them.

Mr. Chester bared his teeth at the cat.

Pavla stopped mid-sentence. She turned. Her mouth fell open. Maddy froze. So did everybody else.

Pavla closed her mouth again. She turned her head away.

From upstairs Maddy heard Anka call out, "Did you hear that?"

"Hear what?" Pavla asked.

"The cat? It's hissing at something," Anka said.

"It's just fussing," Pavla said. "There's nothing there."

Maddy looked at Kazuki and Dimitar, and all of them looked at Pavla, who kept looking in the wrong direction, refusing to see them.

"Thank you," Maddy whispered. She truly meant it.

Pavla didn't say anything.

The cat continued to hiss as Maddy and her friends moved down the passageway, but walked out of their way as they passed the door to the kitchen and crept toward the front door.

Mr. Chester chirped, waving his arms above his head in alarm.

"Wait!" Kazuki said.

Then Maddy heard it too — the witch's car crunching up the gravel driveway.

Mr. Chester scrambled down off Maddy's shoulders and scampered toward a side passage.

"Follow Mr. Chester," Maddy whispered.

The passage led to a laundry room, which had a door that led outside. They ran, and Dimitar waddled, down a short flight of steps to the side of the house.

Maddy risked a peek around the corner of the house, peering through the thick leaves of an overgrown bush. The car had reached the top of the driveway. It followed the small turning circle with the old dead tree in the middle and scrunched to a halt in the gravel. The witch, dressed as Professor Coateloch, was just getting out.

It made Maddy's heart hurt to think that she had trusted this woman. Her parents had trusted this woman enough to let Maddy fly off to a different country with her.

The witch headed toward the front of the house. Maddy waited until she was well inside the house and said, "Hurry!"

She ran. Her feet skidded and slipped on the gravel of the driveway, but she didn't fall. Beside her, Kazuki seemed sure-footed, his nimble black shoes finding stable patches amongst the gravel, while Dimitar waddled along behind and Mr. Chester scampered beside them.

"Where are we going?" Kazuki said right in her ear.

Maddy looked around.

A big SUV was parked at the end of the driveway. It had to be Dimitar's. She crept up to it and tried the door. It was locked. She looked at Dimitar and mimed unlocking it.

Dimitar looked down at the pockets of his pants. It was no use . . . they were covered in thick spiderwebs.

The witch's old black car was parked in front of the house, facing back down the driveway.

The doors were not locked, but there weren't any keys in it.

Kazuki opened the back door of the car. Dimitar leaned into the backseat and somehow shuffled himself across. He twisted and scrunched his knees up to his chest so Maddy could shut the door.

She ran around to the front door, jumped into the driver's seat, and slammed the car door shut behind her. Kazuki got in the other side and quickly went around all the doors, locking them by pushing a small black button.

"Where's the emergency brake?" Kazuki asked.

In her dad's car, Maddy remembered, it was a lever in between the two front seats. But this car didn't have such a lever.

Shouts sounded from the house behind them, followed by crunching footsteps on the gravel. Maddy looked around to see Anka running toward the car. The witch was just coming out of the front door behind her.

Desperately, Maddy looked around the car but could see nothing that looked even similar to the emergency brake in her dad's car.

"There!" Kazuki said, pointing to a D-shaped handle on the dashboard.

Maddy tried to turn it, but it wouldn't move. She pushed it, but it wouldn't go. She tried to pull it, and it came out a little bit.

Anka was right alongside the car now. She tried the handles and yelled at Maddy when she realized they were locked. She banged on the windows.

"Help me!" Maddy cried.

Maddy and Kazuki both pulled on the handle and turned it. It snapped back into the dashboard, and slowly, slowly, the car began to roll.

There was a huge crack from the window behind Maddy, and she looked around to see a large rock in Anka's hand.

The car was moving only at a walking pace, but it was getting faster every second.

Another crack of the rock, and this time the window did break. Broken glass showered Dimitar as he lay on the backseat of the car. He might have been cut if not for the thick mat of webs covering his entire body.

Maddy looked around and saw the witch close behind them. The witch reached into a pocket in her dress and pulled out the car keys on the skull key chain. She pressed a button on the remote control. At the bottom of the driveway, the big metal gates began to close.

Anka's hand reached in the broken window, scrabbling at the black button that locked the door. She pulled it up then let go, reaching for the door handle on the outside of the car.

Before the door could open, however, two little monkey hands reached up and pushed the button back down.

"Good boy, Mr. Chester!" Maddy cried. The car started to roll more quickly through the broken gravestones of the small cemetery. At the bottom of the driveway, the gap between the gates was narrowing.

Anka reached in and pulled the button up again, but as soon as her hand disappeared, Mr. Chester pushed the button back down.

The car was going faster and faster now, and Anka was running alongside, trying to keep up. In front of them, the gates were half closed, with barely enough room for the car to fit between them.

Anka made one last desperate grab for the button and managed to pull it up again, holding onto it this time so Mr. Chester couldn't push it down. She pulled the door open as the car reached the gates.

One of the gates crashed into the car door, slamming it shut. Anka jerked her hand away just in time, then skidded to a halt as the car narrowly slipped through the gap.

"Maddy!" Kazuki yelled.

The car was heading straight toward a huge tree on the other side of the road. Maddy grabbed at the steering wheel, but it was much more stiff and heavy than she had expected. She pulled it around to the right. The car began to turn, but far too slowly.

"Help me!" she yelled, and Kazuki grabbed the wheel as well.

With a spray of gravel, the big car slid around the sharp turn at the end of the driveway and out onto the road, missing the tree by only inches, and gathering speed as it hurtled down the hill through the forest.

"We're going too fast!" Maddy squeaked, twisting the steering wheel a little to the left, a little to the right, struggling to keep the car in the middle of the road. "I can't reach the brakes."

Kazuki let go of the wheel and dropped to the floor.

The car began to slow.

"That's better!" Maddy said.

The car slowed more and more as they came to a small rise in the road.

"We need to go faster," Maddy said.

Kazuki let go of the brake, and the car crawled up the rise, its weight carrying it forward even though the engine wasn't running.

They reached the top and, just as Maddy thought they had completely stopped, they tipped over the brink of the hill, and the car began to move again, slowly, slowly, then a little faster and faster.

"Just say 'brake' when you want to go slower, and I'll press on the brake," Kazuki said.

It was hard keeping the big car in the center of the road. The car veered to the left and the right as she battled with the steering wheel.

Around a sharp corner, there was a thud from the front of the car and a nasty-looking black bird was there: a crow. It was the biggest crow Maddy had ever seen in her life. It was holding onto the windshield wiper with steely claws, peering in with cold bird eyes.

Maddy yelped with fright.

"Don't worry about it! It can't get in," Kazuki said.

But it could. It leaped off the front of the car with a rush of black wings, and next thing she knew, Maddy heard it scraping at the broken back window of the car. It had gripped the bottom of the window with its claws and was trying to pull itself inside.

A screech came from the back of the car. Mr. Chester was hanging from a handle above the window by his tail. He kicked and flailed at the bird with his hands and feet.

There was another, much bigger, thud from the front of the car, and the windshield cracked and shattered into a mosaic of a thousand little glass pieces that bent and bulged but somehow stayed together. In front of Maddy, only an inch or two from her face, were the red-rimmed eyes and the dripping, snarling fangs of a ferocious wolf. It scrambled to grip the hood as it pawed and bit at the shattered windshield of the car.

Another thud, and another wolf joined the first, leaping off a high embankment to their left.

Maddy could barely see where she was going now, with the cracked windshield and two wolves blocking most of her view, but she could tell by the sunlight that suddenly hit the side window that they were emerging from the forest. To the left of the car, there were still tall trees, but when she looked to the right, she could see nothing.

She peered out and down. They were following the narrow road around the side of the mountain. To the right, the road dropped away into a steep ravine.

The wolves bit and pawed at the windshield, a small hole rapidly growing as little shards of glass dropped inside the car.

She hastily steered to the left as they veered dangerously close to the cliff edge. Behind her, Mr. Chester screeched and screamed as he fought off the large black bird.

"Brake!" Maddy yelled as a sharp bend appeared in front of her.

The car slowed and the two wolves on the hood slid away from her toward the front of the car before scrabbling their way back up to the windshield as the car swept around the bend.

Now Maddy could see almost nothing. She struggled and strained for any glimpse of the road ahead. They were speeding down a mountain road with a steep cliff on one side and no idea where they were going.

The hole in the windshield widened more, large enough now for one of the wolves to get a paw inside and reach for her.

She screamed and shuffled as far away as she could without letting go of the steering wheel.

Kazuki's head popped up above the dashboard. He was sitting on the very edge of the seat, pressing on the brake pedal with his foot.

Faster and faster the car rolled, the wind of its passage now blustering inside the car through the hole in the windshield and the broken window where Mr. Chester was still ducking and dodging the sharp beak and claws of the crow.

The wolf with its paw in the windshield moved as it reached out for Maddy, and now she could see, through a clear patch, what was in front of them: a sharp hairpin bend and a deep ravine beyond it.

"Brake!" Maddy yelled, and hauled the steering wheel around to the left.

Kazuki's body went rigid as both of his feet jammed down on the brake pedal.

The tires locked and screamed, and the car turned, sliding sideways toward the flimsy wooden barrier that marked the edge of the cliff.

Now the wolf had its jaws through the hole in the windshield. It snapped at Maddy. Long strings of drool streamed out from its mouth and splashed onto her face. The wolf couldn't reach her yet, but the hole was widening rapidly.

The big car slammed into the barrier with a crunch, and Maddy screamed, certain that they were about to burst through the railings and into the ravine. The railings fractured, slivers of wood flying out over the valley, but somehow, miraculously, the stout posts held.

Maddy was thrown sideways into the door of the car, and Kazuki landed on top of her.

The wolves flew off the car and disappeared over the barrier and down into the ravine.

The car tipped and there was a moment when it seemed to be suspended in midair, and then it began to settle back down. The left wheels landed on the roadway with a thump that shook the entire car, and the car stayed there, crushed up against the barrier but somehow still on the road.

"Wow," breathed Kazuki.

Maddy said nothing. She was quite surprised that they were still alive.

"Mr. Chester!" Kazuki yelled.

Outside the window, Maddy could see the crow flying off over the ravine. That was good. It was leaving them alone.

But it was also terrible — in its claws, the crow held the feeble, struggling body of a little capuchin monkey.

CHAPTER TWENTY-TWO

DRAGON'S TONGUE

AT THE BASE OF THE MOUNTAIN, when the car had finally rolled to a stop, Maddy and Kazuki managed to attract the attention of a truck on the highway. The truck driver, a large lady named Basia, recognized Dimitar immediately. It turned out that she was a big wrestling fan. She cut him free with a box cutter and gave them a lift into town.

Maddy wanted to find a police station and managed to convey that through a basic kind of sign language to Dimitar, but he shook his head and ushered them toward a café on the main street.

The café was empty except for a young waitress with bright pink hair. She came up to the table as soon as they sat down and asked what they wanted. Maddy shook her head at first, but then realized she hadn't eaten since breakfast in the hotel. She was famished. And Kazuki hadn't eaten at all. Maddy ordered a kind of doughnut served with yogurt called *mekitsa* and one for Kazuki as well. By miming, Dimitar let the waitress know that he wanted a cup of coffee. He didn't try to speak.

The waitress disappeared behind the counter.

"We need to go to the police," Maddy said again, and repeated, through miming, to Dimitar. He shook his head and pointed to his lips.

Maddy nodded. He wanted to be able to speak when they tried to explain things to the police.

"Where's the glass tube?" she asked, and Kazuki produced it from somewhere in his suit.

Maddy looked at it. The thin layer of foamlike smoke hid the black shape of the dragon's tongue.

Kazuki shook the tube up a bit.

"Don't do that!" Maddy said.

"Why not?" Kazuki asked.

"I don't know," Maddy said. "It might jumble up all the words."

Dimitar reached out and took the tube from Kazuki. He pulled out the cork. Nothing happened.

He shook the tube like Kazuki had done, but apart from a few whorls and twirls in the smoke, nothing happened.

Eventually, he tipped the tube upside down. The small

piece of dragon's tongue fell out onto the table in front of them and, as it did so, the smoke came out too. Now freed of the tube, it evaporated into a thin cloud around Dimitar's face, and when he breathed in, it disappeared into his mouth and nose. Dimitar looked around, unsure.

"Come on, Dimitar," Maddy said. "Say something." She pointed at her own mouth and flapped it open and shut as if to remind him how to do it.

Dimitar opened his mouth. He counted to five in a voice that sounded rusty and awkward, as though he hadn't used it in a while. His face broke into a huge smile.

"I can speak!" he said.

"That's fantastic!" Maddy said.

"Wonderful!" Kazuki said in Japanese, and Maddy translated for Dimitar.

"It was terrible," Dimitar said. "I couldn't understand anyone, and nobody could understand me."

Kazuki gave her a sad look when she translated that for him, and suddenly she understood: that was every day in Kazuki's world.

Dimitar picked up the piece of dragon's tongue and put it back in the tube, pushing the cork in tightly as if afraid it would somehow steal his voice again. Maddy took the tube and examined it. The top of the tongue was rough and lumpy, a bit like her own when she looked at it in the mirror. It was small, about the size of her little fingernail and not much thicker. The strangest thing was the way it quivered and moved. It gave her the creeps. She put the tube in a pocket where she wouldn't have to look at it.

"Now we must go to the police," Maddy said. She would have jumped up then and there if the waitress hadn't arrived at the table with her and Kazuki's *mekitsi*. They smelled wonderful.

"We have to be very careful what we tell them," Dimitar said. "Perhaps it's best not mention the witch."

"When I told you we'd been kidnapped by a witch, you didn't laugh. You didn't tell me not to be silly," Maddy said.

Dimitar nodded. "But for me, this is not so unusual. My father was a kind of a . . . a magic man. My grandfather also."

"I met your father," Maddy said.

"You did?"

"On a train," Maddy said. "Although it may have been in a dream. He said he would watch out for me."

"But he is gone," Dimitar said. "And he can't look out for you."

"I think he tried," Maddy said.

"How?" Kazuki asked, after Maddy translated for him.

"Mr. Chester," Maddy said. "He's far too clever for a monkey. He's like a little guardian angel." She stopped and dropped her eyes. "Or he *was* like a little guardian angel."

"I will miss my father's monkey," Dimitar said. "I miss them both."

The terrible image came back to Maddy of Mr. Chester struggling in the claws of the crow. She tried to shut it out of her mind, but it made her want to cry.

"Mr. Chester was a good friend," she said.

"But he did fart a lot," Dimitar said.

Maddy laughed.

"Now we must hurry to the police station," Dimitar said. "Before the witch does anything."

"The witch wouldn't dare try anything now, would she?" Maddy asked. "Now we've escaped. We know what she has done and where she is."

"It is because we have escaped that I am afraid," Dimitar said. "She knows we will be going to the police. She knows she will be arrested. She might disappear, or go into hiding, or do something much worse. Who knows what she will do?"

"Then we must go, before it's too late," Maddy said, and repeated it in Japanese for Kazuki.

"It might already be too late," Kazuki said, his eyes wide.

He was staring over Maddy's shoulder out the front window of the café.

"What?" Maddy asked, twisting around to look.

Through the large plate-glass windows, the dark shape of the mountain rose up in front of them. Smoke was pouring from the top of it, and a light yellow mist was spreading out in all directions. It was filtering across the blue of the sky, turning it green and staining the puffy white clouds with an ugly yellow tinge.

"That is the strangest thing." The waitress had just arrived at their table with Dimitar's coffee. She was also peering out the window.

The mist was moving quickly, extending its yellow tentacles out through the sky in all directions.

"It's her," Maddy said. "It's a spell!" Her hand instinctively went to her neck, feeling for the runestone that the witch had said would protect them.

Whatever spell the witch was casting, it was on a much grander scale than before. What had been a wisp of smoke in the witch's lair was now a huge plume of yellow smoke, belching up from the mountain. It looked like a volcano about to erupt.

"I've lived here all my life," the waitress said, "and I have never seen such a strange *urgh* as that before."

"*Urgh?*" Maddy asked.

The waitress looked confused. "I meant mist," she said. "Those mountains often get covered in mist, but not at this time of *kwuffle*. And never a strange yellow *blibblob* like that." She frowned. "I remember one *gwurble* when I was just *befubloodle* and I *globiddy gunga onka onka*."

"It's the tongue spell!" Kazuki said. There was a strange haze in the room now, and Maddy noticed the thin layer of smoke that was curling under the door of the café.

"The smoke," she said. She jumped up and began to stuff paper napkins under the door, but it was clear that she was too late. The smoke was no longer coming into the café. Instead, thick and lumpy, it was seeping back outside.

The waitress had a look of utter confusion. She set the coffee cup on the table, and her hand found her mouth, touching her lips and cheeks as if to make sure they were still there.

"*Bungadoodle quar quar ombo poppa humba homba elbo no no umm mmmm,*" she said.

She covered her mouth with her hands and rushed back behind the counter.

"It's the tongue-taking spell!" Maddy said, in both languages.

"I was afraid the witch would do something like this," Dimitar said. "She's trying to cover her tracks."

"Quickly!" Maddy said. "We must get to the police." They jumped up and ran toward the door.

The police station was a few doors down the street, but a crowd of people, congregating from every direction, surrounded it.

Confusion was spreading and turning to panic. Maddy watched two men fighting outside a barber's shop yelling gibberish at each other. Other people were trying to calm them down and separate them, but they had no words to do so.

Everywhere people were milling around. Some were silent. Perhaps they were afraid to open their mouths for fear of what they might say. Others were shouting nonsense at anyone around them, none of whom, of course, could understand it.

Everybody looked scared and angry.

It occurred to Maddy, at that moment, that apart from the witch and her daughters, she, Kazuki, and Dimitar were possibly the only people in the town who still had the ability to talk to one another. They started to make their way through the crowd toward the police station, and Dimitar pulled Maddy and Kazuki close to him to protect them. As the crowd got thicker, he picked Maddy up and put her on his shoulders like she was a small child. He then picked up Kazuki and held him on his hip with one arm as easily as if he weighed nothing at all.

Maddy looked around at all the commotion and the angry people, and it made her sad. It made her angry, too. Angry at the evil witch who had caused all this.

"Turn around," she said, and Dimitar did. There was no way through and no point anyway. The police, too, would be under the witch's spell by now. How could the police help — how could anyone help — when they couldn't tell them what was going on?

"Ask Dimitar if he has a phone," Kazuki said.

A phone! Why hadn't I thought of that? Maddy wondered. She asked Dimitar, and he quickly produced one from his pocket.

"Can I call my parents?" Maddy asked.

Dimitar nodded. "Of course."

He showed her how to call England, and she dialed the rest of the number herself, but after five or six rings it went to voicemail.

She handed Kazuki the phone. "Try your parents."

"I'll call Dad's cell number," Kazuki said.

He dialed and then put the phone to his ear. Maddy could hear the ringing sound coming from the tiny speaker.

After just a few rings, the phone was answered.

"Dad! Dad!" Kazuki said, then froze, and his face went white.

"What is it?" Maddy asked.

Kazuki lifted the phone away from his ear. Maddy could hear Kazuki's father's voice quite clearly, even if it was a little bit tinny.

"Lordy-doody, muckle boo, ba boomba boomba."

Kazuki tried a couple more times to talk to his father, but after that, Maddy reached out and took the phone from him.

"It's no use," she said. "The spell must be spreading farther and faster than we could possibly have imagined."

"All the way to England?" Kazuki asked.

Maddy rested a hand gently on his arm. "I forgot to tell you — your parents were flying to Bulgaria to look for you. They are here already."

CHAPTER TWENTY-THREE

RECIPE FOR A THUNDERSTORM

THEY LEFT THE CROWD and walked back along the main street. Dimitar stopped suddenly outside a sports shop. He pushed open the door, which jangled an old-fashioned bell inside, and entered.

"What are you doing?" Maddy asked, but Dimitar just gave her a grim look.

The shop was much bigger inside than you would have thought from the small window on the street front. It opened out into a large room filled with sports equipment of all different kinds. The largest displays, near the front, were all for soccer, with balls and shin guards and a variety of shirts from different soccer teams.

There was no sign of a shopkeeper, yet the shop was clearly open, and a cup of coffee was cooling on the counter.

"We have to stop her," Dimitar said, and Maddy knew he was right even though it gave her chills just thinking about it.

She looked at Kazuki, wondering whether to translate Dimitar's words for him. He must have been reading their minds however, because he said it too.

"We have to go back," Kazuki said. "Before midnight."

"Dimitar and I will go back," Maddy said. "You stay here, just in case . . ." She stopped because she couldn't actually think of an "in case," but the last thing she needed was to be worrying about Kazuki when they were heading into such danger.

"I have to come," he said. "I promised to protect you."

"Okay," Maddy said. "You can be our lookout. You can go invisible and keep a lookout to help us stay safe."

"Okay," Kazuki said, and he looked quite relieved. "Can I borrow the phone again?"

Maddy translated, and Dimitar gave him the phone.

Kazuki played around with it for a moment, pressing icons until he found a mapping program. He found their location on the map, then located the witch's house, high in the mountains. He pressed a few more buttons then handed the phone back to Maddy.

Dimitar, watching closely, raised an eyebrow.

"I found the map coordinates for the old house," Kazuki said. "I emailed them to my mom and dad."

"Clever!" Maddy said and explained it to Dimitar.

Dimitar went to the baseball stand. He picked up a wooden bat and swung it a couple of times, single-handed. Happy with the weight and feel of the bat, he picked up another one. Kazuki looked briefly around the shop, then found a pack of baseballs, which disappeared somewhere into his ninja suit.

Dimitar took out his wallet and left some bills on the counter, then walked past the counter to the rear of the shop. A set of car keys was hanging on a hook by the back door. Dimitar picked them up as he passed.

The door led out to a small loading dock. A white van was parked there, and it had the name of the shop emblazoned on its side.

They all sat in the front seat since there was no backseat, and Dimitar drove out of the parking area and along a narrow delivery lane that seemed only just wide enough for the van. He found the highway and turned toward the mountains.

Maddy sat in the middle. The two baseball bats leaning against the seat jostled against her leg as they drove.

"Look at the mountain," Kazuki said.

They all looked. It was different than before, but that was because they could only see half of it. The upper half was hidden by thick black thunderclouds in a perfect ring around the mountain. It was most unusual because the rest of the sky was clear. The clouds roiled and flashed with lightning, and the thunder rolled around them as the van rushed down the highway in that direction.

"That's a strange thunderstorm," Dimitar said.

"She made it," Maddy said softly.

They turned off the highway onto the mountain road and began to climb. Soon they were in the forest, and not long after that, they were in the midst of the thunderstorm as well. Maddy could see the rain in front of them like a curtain across the road. In just one second, the windshield went from totally dry to awash with flowing sheets of water that the wipers did little to clear.

It was as black as night under the thunderstorm, and it was a wonder that Dimitar could see where they were going, Maddy thought. That worried her, especially with the steep drop that she knew was just to the side of them.

Around them, lightning burned the sky. Once, twice, it lit up the inside of the van like a camera flash, then a whole barrage of strikes that sounded like machine-gun fire turned the thunderstorm's night back into day.

Some of the strikes were close, and the dark forest around them exploded momentarily into light as a tree was struck. The air was thick with the strange smell of electricity.

Wind also beat at the van, hammering it one way and then the other as Dimitar fought to keep it in the center of the road. He was driving slowly to avoid driving off the road in the dark, but still Maddy grabbed at the edge of the seat whenever the wind caught the van on a sharp corner. The van tilted up several times, to the point where she thought it might tip over on its side. After a few turns like that, Kazuki's hand crept into hers, and that steadied her.

Still, the rain kept falling, flooding across the windows. In the forest around them, Maddy was conscious of movement. Dark shapes crept amongst the trees and followed the van on its painstaking journey up the hill. Once or twice, Maddy thought she saw the glow of animal eyes reflected in the lightning.

They rounded another sharp corner, and the van suddenly stopped. Maddy peered over the dashboard, trying to see why. It took her a moment to see it, and she wondered how Dimitar had managed to stop in time to avoid a collision.

The branch of a tree had crashed right across the road.

It was huge — from one of the heavy oaks in the forest. The branch was almost a tree in itself. The scorched end showed why it had fallen.

Dimitar started to open the door of the van, and rain sprayed inside, propelled by the wind. Then there was an eerie noise.

"Wolves!" Maddy cried, and Dimitar paused and then picked up one of the baseball bats before opening the door again.

"This is the horn," he said, and pressed the middle of the steering wheel. It made a long beep. He looked back at them and said, "If you see a wolf, sound the horn."

Dimitar got out of the car, mindless of the teeming rain that soaked him in a second. His long hair plastered down over his head, and his beard ran a river down his chest. He strode toward the fallen branch, the baseball bat held firmly in one hand. He scanned the forest around him, but when no wolves, or crows, or animals, or birds of any kind emerged, he put the bat on the ground within easy reach and began to pull on the branch.

Maddy rested her hand lightly on the horn, trying to watch everywhere at the same time. She thought she saw movement in the trees to the right of where Dimitar was working. She almost pressed the horn, but Dimitar had heard it or seen it as well. He let go of the branch and picked up the bat, waiting and watching for a moment. Nothing came into view. It might have been the wind.

He put the bat back down and resumed hauling the heavy branch.

Maddy doubted if any normal man could have moved the branch at all, but Dimitar hauled it right to the side of the road, clearing a path before climbing back into the van.

"Are you okay?" Maddy asked. "You're all wet."

"It's just water," Dimitar said. He wiped his face with a grimy hand that left smears of mud down his face and made him look even more fearsome than before.

They drove carefully past the fallen branch and rounded another corner.

The hillside dropped away to the left and now, across a small valley, they could see the dark walls and wicked spires of the witch's hideaway.

Maddy shuddered and felt Kazuki shrink down in the seat beside her. Seeing that house, appearing and reappearing like a mirage through the sheets of rain that fell into the valley, made her want to turn and run away.

They emerged from the rain as suddenly as they had entered it. One moment they were being lashed by gushes of water and the next they were driving under a cloudless sky, rapidly darkening with the approach of night. Out across the valley now, they could see the storm, a giant ring around the mountain. It was still flashing and thundering amidst the turbulent clouds but was clear in the center.

The storm wasn't done with them yet though, and just as the road turned sharply back toward the storm, there was another huge burst of light and a simultaneous crash of thunder. An entire oak tree was falling out of the storm front right before their eyes, its mighty trunk cleaved by the terrible swift sword of lightning.

Dimitar slammed on the brakes, and the tires of the van screamed on the dry road. It veered sideways to a halt as the tree crashed down in a maelstrom of leaves and branches just in front of them.

The van rocked on its suspension, just a couple inches from the cliff edge.

They all sat still, breathing deeply, staring at the tree trunk that now blocked the road.

Not even a giant like Dimitar was going to be able to move that whole oak tree by himself.

"I think we are walking the rest of the way," Dimitar said in a low, angry voice.

Kazuki was the first to open his door. He climbed down and looked up at Maddy.

Dimitar was already stepping out of the van on the other side, both baseball bats clenched in one giant fist.

Maddy climbed down on Kazuki's side and pushed the van door closed behind her. Around them, the forest made forest noises and every one of them seemed full of danger and dread.

Dimitar stepped up to the fallen tree and found a place near the base of the trunk where the branches were not so thick. He stepped one foot over and straddled the tree, then lifted each of the children over.

"Walk behind me," he said.

The leaves of the trees were moving around them, and this time it was not the wind. There were definite movements in the trees. Animals were tracking them as they walked. Fierce eyes peered at them out of the shadows. A raucous call sounded from the sky above them, and Maddy looked up to see a trio of black crows circling.

"Look," Kazuki said. The moon was up, low on the horizon — big, bright, and orange. That wasn't what Kazuki was looking at, though. It was the thick yellow smoke, heavy and lumpy, drifting toward them.

The tongues of hundreds of thousands — maybe millions — of people were starting to arrive as the witch's spell took hold and spread farther and farther.

CHAPTER TWENTY-FOUR

THE STROKE OF MIDNIGHT

IT WAS A LONG WAY UP the mountain, and although they ran and walked as fast as they could, it was almost midnight before they finally arrived at the straight stretch of road that led to the gates of the old black house.

The road ran alongside a high wall, unmarked except at one place where a tree branch had fallen onto the wall, cracking the stone at the top.

The gates were shut. Maddy had expected that, but actually to see it as they approached made her worry a little more. How would they get in? The gates were high and topped with sharp spikes. The wall was even higher and, although old and grimy, it was as smooth as glass to the touch with no handholds or footholds to climb.

As they approached the gates, they could hear chanting coming from inside. Kazuki pulled over his ninja mask and crept to the gates, crouching near the ground and poking his head slowly around the corner. After a moment, he motioned to the others to come up. Maddy kneeled down and peered past the large stone gatepost, just above where he was crouching, and Dimitar put his head above them both.

An almost full moon shined down on the house, washing everything with burnished silver. In the garden, a bonfire added a yellow-orange glow. It was in a cleared area in the middle of the cemetery, and it crackled and spat sparks over the broken tombstones that surrounded it. The bonfire was tall: higher than the witch and her daughters who pranced and chanted in a circle around it. The light from the moon and the glow of the fire reflected off the almost-bald head of the witch, and her thick black ponytail danced about as if it had a life of its own.

The witch had a wooden pail in one hand and took ladlefuls of a yellow liquid from it, tossing it into the flames, where it fizzed and popped. Each time she did, a thick plume of dark yellow smoke puffed up and out of the bonfire into a small mushroom-shaped cloud before drifting up higher in the air, coloring the stars as it went.

On a stand near the fire was a huge glass jar. It was as big as an old-fashioned wooden barrel. Inside the jar, a

black shape writhed and squirmed. Not a mere morsel of dragon's tongue — it seemed to Maddy that this was an entire tongue.

Black and awful and somehow still alive, it seemed to be trying to escape. But the glass sides were sheer, and the tongue could only squirm around in the thick yellow mist that was condensing in the base of the jar. The sight of the tongue made a cold shiver run down Maddy's spine, but the knowledge that every tiny wisp of smoke in the jar was the voice, the language, the "tongue" of some poor person, made hot bile rise up inside her. How dared the witch do this?

There was no way in. No way to stop her. Even if Maddy was small enough to squeeze through the gates, there was no way for Dimitar to do so, and what could one girl, not yet ten years old, do against a witch and her teenage daughters?

Dimitar crept back from the gates and motioned for them to join him so they could talk without risk of being heard.

"How does she open the gates?" he asked. "Is it magic?"

"It's science," Maddy replied. "She has a gate opener on a key chain in a pocket in her dress."

"Back down there is a branch of a tree fallen onto the

wall," Dimitar said. "If I lift you up on top of the wall, do you think you could climb down the tree on the other side?"

"I think so," Maddy said, then explained Dimitar's suggestion to Kazuki.

"I should go with you," Kazuki said.

"No," Maddy said. "We need you here to be our lookout."

Kazuki was terrified of heights, and anyway, Maddy didn't want to be worrying about him once she was inside. "I will try to sneak the key chain out of her pocket, then open the gates and let you both in."

Kazuki shook his head. "Not you. It has to be me. I'm the one who can go invisible."

"Kazuki," Maddy said. "You don't really go invisible."

"I know that," he said. "But if I'm careful and quiet, it's like being invisible. Nobody seems to see me."

"No," Maddy said, and her voice made it clear that that was that. "I'll do it. We need you as a lookout."

She dashed back to where the branch of the tree protruded over the wall.

Dimitar lifted Maddy, grabbing her by the ankles and hoisting her right up until she could scramble on top of the wall.

The branch was thick but appeared rotten. She hoped it was strong enough to bear her weight. There was only one way to find out.

Maddy stretched out her hands like a tightrope walker and took one step. The branch was smooth and round. It sagged a little under her weight but held.

Looking only at the tree trunk in front of her, she took one tentative step after another along the branch. She almost made it. In fact, she would have if not for the cat.

She was almost across to the tree, and safety, when there was a harsh hissing noise close to her head. She looked up in fright to see two eyes — one dark, the other green — reflecting the light of the bonfire in the graveyard beyond. The cat snarled and clawed at her and, although it was well out of reach, it made Maddy flinch and slip. She recovered but leaned too far the other way, swaying and wobbling, trying to get her balance back. She started to fall. She clutched at the branch, wrapping her arms and legs around it and sliding underneath, staring at the ground, which suddenly seemed a very long way down.

Something grabbed at her neck, and she realized it was the cord of her runestone necklace snagged on a jagged piece of bark. It snapped, and the runestone dropped away to the dark ground below.

She clawed desperately at the soft wood of the rotten branch. Pieces of bark came away from underneath her fingers, and her hands slipped even more. She struggled not to cry out, knowing that any loud noise would alert the witch.

Her other hand slipped, then a large piece of wood came away, and suddenly she was falling!

But a steely grip wrapped around her wrist as she fell, and instead of tumbling to the ground, she swung into the trunk of the tree with a *whumph* that knocked all the air out of her body. Her foot found a branch, then her free hand found another one, and she was safe amongst the branches. She looked up to see Kazuki, his face whiter than snow, lying on top of the branch with his arms and legs wrapped around it. He was small, but she had never realized before how strong he was. He let go of her wrist when he saw she was safe.

"Kazuki!" she said. She had told him not to come, but he had come anyway. To keep her safe.

The acid hissing of the cat came from just above her head, and she looked up to see it was on the next branch up. It wasn't hissing at her but at Kazuki, who was sitting up, staring at the cat.

Kazuki held one of the baseballs he had taken from the

sports shop. He tossed it up a couple of times in one hand, then drew back his arm.

The cat turned and disappeared down the tree.

With Maddy safe, Kazuki put away the baseball and began to inch his way along the branch. When he got to the safety of the main trunk, he stopped, shaking uncontrollably.

The climb down the tree was easier. Maddy helped Kazuki, showing him where to put his hands and feet. The tree had many branches, and it was almost like a staircase, except for when they reached the bottom and had to jump the last several feet. Kazuki did it with his eyes shut, and Maddy helped steady him as he landed.

"Thank you, Kazuki," she said.

He was breathing so heavily that Maddy was afraid the witch would hear, but he sucked in enough air to say, "I'll go get the key chain."

Maddy hesitated. "Okay, but be careful," she said. "I'll do something to distract them."

Kazuki nodded, pulled over his hood, and right before her eyes, he melted away into the deep shadow by the wall. Even though she knew where he was, it took a concentrated effort to see him in his black ninja suit.

From within the old house she heard the sound of a

clock. The old grandfather clock. It began to chime the hours. It was midnight!

The witch started to chant again, horrible words in a sinister old language. Deep down, Maddy felt that this was somehow her fault. She was the one who had translated the spells. She had told the witch she would call the police. But what else could she have done? Maddy clutched at her neck, remembering the runestone that had dropped. She looked around for it, but a dark stone on the dark ground at night was going to take too long to find — if she could find it at all.

Maddy ran toward the bonfire. She was out of the trees now, among the old stones of the cemetery. She no longer cared about being seen. She wanted to be seen.

She thought of Kazuki risking his life, climbing out along the broken tree branch despite his terrible fear of heights. She thought of Dimitar, huge and powerful, but brought to his knees by the witch's spells. She thought of the waitress at the café and all the people in the town who could no longer speak. Of Kazuki's mom and dad babbling on the phone. She no longer cared what happened to her.

She ran, her fists clenched, her hair standing on end, her voice half a shout, half a scream.

"Stop it!" she screamed. "Stop it, you ugly witch!"

The witch stopped chanting. The girls stopped dancing. Even the fire seemed to stop crackling and popping for a moment as this red-headed apparition, shaking and running and screaming out of the trees, came toward them.

"Maddy," the witch snarled.

"You're so ugly that your doctor is a vet!" Maddy yelled, her cheeks burning. "You're so ugly you make onions cry!"

From inside the house she heard the clock continue to chime the hour.

Two.

A few seconds more, and the stolen tongues would turn to dust.

"Get her," the witch said quite calmly and turned back to the bonfire. The light from it shimmered off her velvety chocolate dress and lit her hair from behind, making it glow.

"When you were born, your doctor took one look at you and slapped your parents!" Maddy yelled.

The witch ignored her. Behind the witch, silhouetted by the light of the fire, she could see a dark shape and a small hand reaching out toward the witch's pocket.

Three.

"I know who you are, Professor Coateloch," Maddy cried out, just as Anka reached her. She should have turned and tried to run, but fury was burning inside her, brighter than the bonfire. Anka's hand clamped down on her arm, and then she was being dragged back toward the witch.

The witch cackled. "Professor Coateloch? There is no Professor Coateloch. If your parents had bothered checking with the university, they could have found that out. But they were too busy counting their money. They sold you, Maddy. They sold you for a thousand dollars. That's all you were worth."

Maddy struggled, tears in her eyes, but she couldn't break Anka's grip.

"What's this?" the witch screamed, and her hand now grasped a small wrist — Kazuki's wrist. In Kazuki's hand were the keys and the opener for the gate. He cried out in pain, and the keys dropped to the ground.

Four.

"Small boys and girls do make delightful eating," the witch cackled again, "but they have to be cooked first." She pulled Kazuki closer to the fire.

"Leave him alone!" Maddy shouted.

The witch ignored her, and now Anka was dragging Maddy, too, closer and closer to the roaring bonfire.

"Leave her alone!" It was Pavla's voice. She gripped Maddy by the other arm.

"Pavla!" the witch shrieked.

Pavla looked at her mother, and her face shrank, but she did not let go of Maddy's arm.

Five.

"Leave them alone!" Dimitar yelled. He thrust his arms through the railings as if he could somehow reach them from there. He rattled the gates, but even his giant strength was no match for the huge metal bars.

Six.

The tug of war continued with Maddy in the middle. Pavla was bigger and stronger, but Anka was more determined. The fire loomed closer. Maddy could feel the heat on her face and bare arms now.

The witch had stopped cackling and was talking — whispering a spell that Maddy remembered from the ancient scrolls. Her fingertips began to glitter.

"Look out, Dimitar!" she screamed.

Behind Dimitar one of the huge oaks of the forest was hauling its own roots up out of the ground. It pulled itself along the ground using the roots like arms. The top of the tree wavered and tottered as it moved.

The witch was calling the tree.

Seven.

Dimitar turned, but the tree was already upon him,

giant oak branches reaching out for him, trapping him against the metal gates.

"Dimitar!" Maddy screamed again. Now the fire was just in front of her face, and she could feel her eyebrows start to singe from its heat. She turned her face away from the flames. Nothing could help them now, nothing short of a miracle. Then she saw it.

The key chain with the gate opener on it was still lying on the ground where Kazuki had dropped it. As she watched, a tiny hand reached for it. A smaller-than-human hand — smaller, even, than that of a baby. It was the hand of a little monkey, hiding in the folds of the witch's cloak.

"Mr. Chester!" Maddy cried. The little hand pressed the green button on the gate opener, and with a creak and a groan the big metal gates began to open.

Eight.

"What?" the witch cried and looked down.

Mr. Chester jumped out from the folds of the cloak. He looked different somehow and later, when Maddy had time to think about it, she would realize that it was the crow's feather stuck on a jaunty angle in the hatband of his tiny hat. He looked up at the witch with a sly grin and gathered up the keys, scampering off with them.

"Get him!" the witch shouted. Anka let go of Maddy's

arms and chased after the monkey. Pavla was still pulling, and she and Maddy went over in a heap.

Dimitar was already out of the clutches of the tree and storming across the yard toward the witch.

Nine.

The witch let go of Kazuki. Her eyes rolled back in her head, and her fingertips began to glitter once more.

Another spell. A spell of spiders, or centipedes, or lightning, or, Maddy feared, something much worse.

The anger inside Maddy was gone now. A calmness came over her, and she suddenly knew what she had to do. She untangled herself from Pavla and jumped up. She saw Kazuki scrambling on his hands and knees away from the witch, away from the fire. She saw the jar, full of the tongues of people about to be trapped forever.

"Kazuki! The jar!" she yelled.

Ten.

He must have been thinking the same thing because there was a loud bang, and a huge crack appeared in the jar as a baseball bounced off it and rolled away somewhere amongst the gravestones. The crack spread like a spiderweb across the glass, but the jar remained intact.

Maddy closed her eyes, remembering the words of the old scrolls. She opened them again and began to chant.

Kazuki drew a second baseball out of his ninja suit and drew his arm back, a tense, taut spring. But what he hadn't seen, what Maddy hadn't seen either, was Anka, hurtling down on Kazuki from behind, her fingers rigid, like the talons of a hunting bird, her lips drawn back from her teeth like a vicious dog.

Kazuki took aim just as Anka leaped into the air behind him, but with a thud that Maddy felt from a few feet away, the witch's daughter went flying off to the side, away from Kazuki. The much larger shape of Pavla was on top of her, pinning her sister to the ground.

Kazuki's arm snapped forward, and the ball hurtled toward the already cracked glass. There was a splintering sound, and the ball smashed right through the side of the jar. The jar broke into two large pieces. One of them toppled off the stand and smashed into even smaller pieces on the ground. The dragon's tongue flopped out of the wreckage of the jar and landed amongst the shards of glass, still writhing and jerking.

The thick yellow smoke drifted up into the air, evaporating into a long, pale cloud that got thinner and thinner as it rose higher, and the trapped tongues began the journey back to their owners.

Eleven.

Maddy's own fingertips began to flash as magic welled up inside her and burst out through her hands like sparklers. She grasped a burning branch from the fire and threw it on the ground at the witch's feet. A cloud of the yellow smoke rose up, enveloping the witch, who scarcely seemed to notice, so great was her concentration on the storming giant who was approaching her.

The ground in front of Dimitar began to soften as the witch chanted her spell, and he started to slow, each footstep sinking deeper and deeper into the earth. In a moment, Maddy knew, the earth would swallow her big friend entirely, but she didn't let herself think about that.

Her hand found the glass tube in her pocket, and she pulled it out, removing the stopper as she continued to chant the words of the spell exactly as she had read it in the old parchment scrolls.

Twelve!

Her arms flopped to her sides, the sparks from her fingertips dying away to fizzles and pops and then to a gentle glitter. She swayed on her feet, totally exhausted.

The witch continued to chant, but her words were no longer the incantations of ancient magic. *"Bummity boodle, gwurgle,"* the witch said.

The sparks in the witch's fingertips died.

"Blaggedy bong, budda budda gunga doodle."

The ground beneath the giant began to firm, and he strode steadily forward.

Maddy looked at the glass tube in her hand, noticing in a dizzy, dazed kind of way that a thick yellow smoke — the tongue of the witch — was settling down inside. She pushed the stopper back into the tube.

"Hubbidy hobbidy blurble bab," the witch said, her eyes wide with fear. Dimitar was right in front of her, and he clamped one hand over the witch's mouth, although Maddy knew that was no longer necessary.

The witch had not worn a runestone — as the caster of the spell, she was immune from its powers. But she was no longer the caster of the spell — Maddy was — and as the clock struck midnight and one day turned into the next, it was the witch herself who lost her tongue.

The glittering from Maddy's fingertips faded and as it did, so did the sky and the bonfire and the witch, and Dimitar and Kazuki and the entire world was just a cloud. The world was reeling around her now, and in the middle of it all was the bonfire, a huge, bright, burning light, growing and getting hotter. Maddy was falling toward the heat, and it was burning, and then it all faded away.

CHAPTER TWENTY-FIVE

THE HELICOPTER

MADDY WOKE TO THE SOUND of birds singing in the trees. Not the harsh caw of crows, but the lyrical lullabies of thrushes and the cheerful cooing of pigeons.

She was on the floor of one of the rooms of the old house, on a rough mattress that had been made for her from cushions taken from the sofa. Dimitar's jacket had been pulled over her as a blanket, and she was grateful for it; the morning was cold.

When she sat up, she saw Kazuki lying on one of the sofas. He looked like he had just woken up too. His hair was sticking out in every direction.

"What happened?" she asked.

"You passed out," Kazuki said, sitting up on the sofa. "You almost fell in the fire. You would have if . . ." He stopped, not wanting to say more, but Maddy guessed. It was Kazuki who had rushed over and caught her as she had fallen toward the flames.

"Thank you, Kazuki," she said, but those three words could not really tell him how she was feeling. No words could. Not in any language.

"Thank *you*," he said in return. "You saved us all. Turning the spell back on the witch was brilliant."

There was a sudden scampering of tiny feet, and Mr. Chester bounded into the room, jumping up onto Maddy's shoulders and rubbing his hands vigorously through her hair.

"All right, all right." Maddy giggled. "I'm glad to see you too."

He hopped down and sat in her lap. The crow feather in his hat stuck out like a badge of courage. Whether he had stuck it there himself, or whether it had just ended up there during his fight with the crow, nobody would ever know. But it stayed.

On a small table next to her was the glass tube with the witch's tongue: her language, her spells, trapped inside forever.

Mr. Chester cocked his head, listening, and then began to hop up and down on Maddy's lap, clearly excited about something.

"Listen," Kazuki said.

After a moment, Maddy heard it too. The rapidly approaching *chop, chop* sound of a helicopter. She sprang to her feet, and Mr. Chester had to leap for her neck to stop himself from being thrown halfway across the room, so sudden was her movement.

"Come on," she said. She ran into the kitchen. There, tied to chairs with bindings made from ripped up bedsheets were the witch and her two daughters.

The witch glared at Maddy as she entered.

"Rubble bubble," she said. *"Flirty wap."*

"Flirty wap to you, too," Maddy said with a cheery smile.

Anka looked furious, but Pavla seemed sad and frightened.

Maddy winked at Pavla to let her know that things would be all right.

With Mr. Chester on her shoulder and Kazuki close behind, Maddy walked outside.

Dimitar was already out there, looking up at the sky with a hand shielding his eyes from the glare of the morning sun.

"Here's our brave girl," he said. "How are you this morning?"

"Rubble bubble," Maddy said. *"Flirty wap."* As Dimitar was starting to look worried, she added, "That's what the witch just said to me. I'm fine, thank you very much."

Dimitar chuckled, a deep, throaty laugh, and said, "I'm pleased to hear it."

Maddy saw the helicopter flying low through the valley.

It hovered for a few seconds, then settled gently into a large, clear area to the left of the graveyard.

For some reason Maddy expected it to be full of police, but instead, to her great surprise, the first person to step down out of the helicopter was her mom and then her dad. Then came Kazuki's parents, and perhaps the greatest surprise of all was the person who came out last. She recognized the smile beaming from the shadows inside the helicopter before she even saw the bald head and soft eyes of William Buthelezi, the Zulu speaker who had been on TV with her.

"Mom!" Maddy squealed and ran toward her mom, who ran as fast toward Maddy. Her hair a mess, she was crying, and she picked up Maddy in a giant bear hug. Her dad wrapped his arms around them both and was laughing and laughing and laughing.

"What? How?" Maddy asked as soon as she was able to get her breath back.

Her mom set her down on the ground but wasn't about to let her go yet.

She saw that Kazuki's parents had him in just the same kind of hug, and they weren't about to let go either.

"Mr. Buthelezi, as it turns out, is very, very rich," Maddy's dad said. "A millionaire, in fact. When he heard you were missing, he called and offered to help. He flew us here to Bulgaria in his private jet, and we joined Kazuki's parents to look for you. But we didn't know where to find you until Kazuki's dad got the message with the GPS map of this house."

"Thank you," Maddy said to William Buthelezi, who gave a short bow from the waist.

"I told you that if you ever wanted my help, it was yours, and I meant it," he said.

"When we got the map, Mr. Buthelezi tried to charter a helicopter," her dad continued. "But then everybody suddenly forgot how to talk, and we couldn't do anything."

"It was most strange," William said. "Everybody just started babbling like newborn babies."

"Including us!" her mom said. "But when we woke up this morning, everything was back to normal. So Mr. Buthelezi hired the helicopter, and we came here as fast as we could."

"What happened here?" Kazuki's dad asked in Japanese.

Maddy translated the question for the others, first in English, then in Bulgarian for Dimitar.

"That's a very long story," she said.

"Well, you can tell us later," Maddy's mom said. "I'm so happy to have you back."

She hugged Maddy again, then hugged Dimitar for helping save her, and she hugged William for all his help, and she hugged Kazuki's mom and dad because she was so pleased that Kazuki was safe and sound also, then she hugged Maddy again, and Maddy hugged her back.

Maddy's mom even asked her how to say "thank you" in Bulgarian and in Zulu and spent the next few minutes thanking them both over and over again in their own languages (although with a terrible accent!).

Mr. Chester had disappeared somewhere while all this hugging was going on, but now he came scampering back, running up Maddy's arm and perching on her shoulder. He put both his arms around her neck for a moment then let go and gave her a quick little peck on the cheek.

"Eww, monkey kiss," Maddy said, but she was smiling. Mr. Chester kissed her again, then leaped off her shoulder onto the arm of Dimitar, running up and perching on his shoulder.

"Goodbye, Mr. Chester," Maddy said, and the monkey saluted once again like a soldier.

The first police car arrived not long after that, and sitting next to the driver was Inspector Teodorov, who looked greatly relieved to see Maddy and Kazuki safe and sound. More police cars arrived and so did more helicopters with cameras and TV news crews. It was all turning into quite a circus, Maddy thought.

In the midst of it all, she found Kazuki sitting on a dining chair, one of a number of which had been dragged outside the house for people to sit on. He seemed to be enjoying all the attention, even if he understood very little of it. Maddy sat next to him and put her arm around his shoulder.

"Thank you, Kazuki," she said. "We wouldn't be here if not for you."

"It's all thanks to you," Kazuki said.

"I think you are one of the bravest, strongest people I have ever met," Maddy said. "And I think you'd make a great ninja warrior."

Kazuki tilted his face toward hers and smiled. He said nothing, but he didn't need to. There was a different look in his eyes now, and Maddy knew that things would be different for him from now on.

THE END